9 780999 446294

Aldous Huxley's

# 34 STORIES

Selected Stories from the 2020
Literary Taxidermy Short Story Competition

Edited by

MARK MALAMUD

## 34 STORIES / 124 BELOVED

All stories © 2020 by their respective authors
Introduction © 2020 by Mark Malamud
Anthology © 2020 by Regulus Press
Cover art "In Stitchu" © 2020 by Len Peralta *after Harry Barton*

First Regulus Press printing November 2020
Signal Library 10-0202-12-01

Regulus Press, Seattle WA
*www.regulus.press*

ISBN: 0999446294
ISBN-13: 978-0-9994462-9-4
(Regulus Press)

**A squat grey building of only thirty-four stories.**
↓
**South-south-west, south, south-east, east....**

—Aldous Huxley, first and last line from *Brave New World*

# CONTENTS

# Introduction

Welcome to *34 Stories*, the anthology (this side up) that collects the ten prize-winning stories from the Aldous Huxley contest of the 2020 Literary Taxidermy Short Story Competition. (If you're looking for the Toni Morrison contest, you'll need to flip this book over and upside-down.)

Literary taxidermy is a story-writing process that involves taking the first and last sentence from a well-known work (often a novel, sometimes a short story) and then "re-stuffing" what goes in-between those lines to create a new, wholly-original work. The goal of the literary taxidermist is not just to slap someone else's words onto the start and finish of an otherwise stand-alone story, but to take full ownership of the borrowed lines, interpreting (or re-interpreting) them in order to make them seamless, integral, and in fact the *perfect* start and finish for a *new* story.

The origin of literary taxidermy is *The Gymnasium*, a collection of nineteen stories written between 2003 and 2017 that "re-stuff" classic works by Richard Brautigan, Milan Kundera, Virginia Woolf, and others. It was a clear example of creative parsimony on the part of the author (some might call it laziness), leveraging the words of other writers to jump-start the creative process. Yet rather than ending up as a pastiche or spoof of other (granted, far better) writers, the stories turned out to be very much their own thing. And it made one wonder: What would happen if rather than having a single writer tackle the first and last lines of a variety of classic works, you had a *variety* of writers tackle the *same* lines? What would that collection be like?

Which brings us to the anthology you hold in your hands and the competition that produced it. The Literary Taxidermy Short Story Competition, sponsored for the third year by Regulus Press, invites writers to stitch together their own stories using the opening and closing sentences of specific works of fiction. For the 2018 competition, participants were given three choices: *The Thin Man* written by Dashiell Hammett; *Through the Looking-Glass* by Lewis Carroll; or "A Telephone Call" by Dorothy Parker. For the 2019 competition, co-edited with Paul Van Zwalenburg, they were given *Fahrenheit 451* by Ray Bradbury.

This year, for the 2020 competition, aspiring writers were given two choices: Aldous Huxley's *Brave New World* and Toni Morrison's *Beloved*.

The present anthology (this side up) contains stories from the Huxley contest. That means that every story you're about to read starts and ends *exactly* the same way—with the first and last lines of *Brave New World*. Of course *the path* that each author takes from beginning to end is unique—and therein lies a particular thrill of reading these short works: despite sharing a common frame, they are all *different*.

So some of the stories in this collection are funny, some are serious, some are heart-warming, some are scary, and some are just *strange*. They cross genres; they cross continents (and occasionally planets); and they vary in style and diction and tone and voice. Reading each one is like getting a peek at the results of someone else's Rorschach test.

The authors are eclectic, too. They range in age from twenty-five to sixty-two. They also span the globe, so you're about to read stories from the United Kingdom, the United States, Ireland, Australia, New Zealand, Canada, and Sweden. (And that's why you may notice stories written in British and American English—so don't be shocked to find *colour* in one story and *color* in the next.) The winning author in this year's Huxley contest is Amanda la Bas de Plumetot, a cinema worker in Melbourne, Australia. Her submission, "Cornucopia," tells a story of love and necessity, set in a world of cultural disparity that is simultaneously primitive, futuristic, and surreal.

But there's more to these stories than the pleasure found in their distinction or their differences. Their *similarities* can be just as intriguing.

Yes, you will find a number of stories within this collection built upon architecture—after all, the opening line is *A squat grey building of only thirty-four stories*.

And the last line—*South-west, south-south-west, south, south-east, east*—guarantees there are numerous tales that spin around the cardinal directions.

But *those* similarities are not particularly interesting. What's interesting are the similarities that appear in story after story that are *unexpected*. For example, this contest received a statistically-improbable number of stories that include mini-skirts, death (or worse) in hotels, and vodka martinis. Why? What is it about *those* two lines by Aldous Huxley that trigger *these* particular narrative neurons to fire?

Literary taxidermy is nothing if not a kind of inkblot test, an invitation to interpret and then riff inside an ambiguous narrative frame. Even if the bizarre similarities that emerge are inexplicable (and really: why *do* so many of the Huxley stories concern mini-skirts?), it shouldn't be a shock that the same input yields similar output. And yet the black box in-between—the human imagination—remains a mystery.

The stories in both anthologies (this one, right-side up, and that one, upside down) were selected by the editors at Regulus Press. The two winning stories were selected by a panel of eight professional-writer judges. After each story, you'll find a short biographical note about the author, and maybe—just maybe—*you* can figure out how they ended up writing the story they did!

Mark Malamud
5 October 2020

## Thomas Baldwin

# The Crystal Tower

A SQUAT GREY BUILDING of only thirty-four stories was not what Chira had had in mind when her father had distributed the districts among her and her brothers, but it would do for now. She was not planning on being there long, anyway.

Her private quarters took up the top three floors. The previous occupant had had a thing for brutalism, but all the plain white walls and angular furniture was too ascetic for her. She selected the French Rococo setting and watched as tapestries rolled down the walls, and the right-angled chairs coiled into ornately-carved *chaises longues*.

On her first night she lined up all her sector managers under the age of 50, selected the best-looking one, and took him to bed. His name was Galan-something. The scars on his back were old, which meant he wielded the whip now. They drank perfect reproduction champagne and had sex on a replica of Louis XV's bed.

Afterwards, she led him up the spiral staircase into her observatory on the roof. She could have set the sixteen glass walls to show any scene at all, but she liked to look out on the reality: hundreds of miles of conveyor belts and gantries, criss-crossing each other, web-like, across mines hundreds of feet deep; the miners like termites; chimneys throwing up gouts of smoke which dyed the sky sunset-red all day.

"Beautiful, isn't it?" she said. "All that activity. But it could be even better."

"Your father hasn't complained," he murmured.

"The old man's losing his touch. The shareholders will put him out of his misery soon enough."

"Is that why you and your brothers have all been given districts?"

She pointed. "Alak to the east, Gethlan to the south-east, Sondalar to the south, Fettal to the west. All in bigger palaces than this one."

"Does that bother you?"

She drained her champagne glass and tried to refill it, but the bottle was empty. She tossed it into the corner, where it landed with a disappointing thud. "It means I'm expected to fail."

She looked out over the Hadean landscape. "But if I can make a success of this place, the shareholders will put me in charge of the whole company."

Most of the first two floors of the palace consisted of a reception hall, with a balcony round three sides. She'd toyed with "conference centre" but eventually decided "19th Century theatre" was more impressive, complete with three-tier crystal chandelier, red velvet curtains, and intricate gilded decoration. Seven-hundred and fifty chairs, filled with managers and workforce representatives from every sector, faced a stage on which Chira sat with half a dozen senior executives and a large, nervous-looking man in a blue boiler-suit.

She stood and approached the dais. As she opened her mouth, she knew her voice would be crackling through the mine shafts and ringing out across factory floors, loud enough to be heard over the district's machinery. She said she would make the district a place to be proud of, and that everyone who worked hard would share in its success. She promised rewards for the most productive individuals and departments: money, fresh food, better quarters, pardons for family members in prison.

"And now," she said, "it gives me great pleasure to

present my first worker-of-the-week award to Sirren, a miner from Sector 73, who has broken all output records this week." She beckoned, and Sirren stood up and approached her. He was sweating, and clutched his cap in both hands. He had made an effort to clean himself, but there was still red dust under his fingernails.

"Sirren, you are a perfect example of the dedication we need in this district. I'm delighted to present you with this certificate, and as promised you will find an extra thousand credits in your account this week."

She held out her hand, and he shook it as applause rippled round the room. He made to pull back, but she held on to him.

"I also have a surprise. I'm told you and your wife have had the maximum number of children, but they have all died. You were on the waiting list for another slot, but—as we all know—that is a long list.

"Well, today, I'm delighted to announce that we have moved you up the queue and granted you reproductive rights for another child."

The applause swelled. Sirren cried.

She asked them to pick a sector they knew was doing well, for a surprise inspection. "I don't want anything ugly to happen, but I need them to know that I can appear anywhere," she said.

She refused a mask at first, but one breath of the unfiltered air outside the palace drove her back in, coughing violently and gasping for breath.

"How can people live in this?" she asked as they went back out again, her face covered. "I guess you must have adapted to cope."

No one said anything.

She walked down the wide steps outside the palace's grand entrance, past the line of soldiers, and into the waiting hovercar, glancing back at the two-storey high image of her face above the main door.

As the vehicle set off, it passed a large area of dirty grass and stunted trees. A few off-duty families were sitting with picnics. "What's this area called?" Chira asked.

Her senior assistant, a woman a little older than she called Palla, glanced over. "It's just The Field. People use it for recreation."

Chira drummed her fingers on the car door. "I think we should have some sort of monument there," she said. "A big tower. Marking the rebirth of this district."

Palla looked apprehensive. "That…may be unpopular. It's the only open area available to most families in the central sector."

Chira ignored her. "I want detailed plans by next week, and the ground broken the week after that."

The road dropped into the private tunnel network for executives, and it went dark outside, except for brief glimpses of more industrial vistas: vats of molten metal and men striking up sparks with massive hammers. The car stopped at a sector administrative office. As Chira stepped out, the manager burst through the door, hurriedly straightening her cap. "Madam President," she spluttered, "I'm Fadellan. We're honoured."

"Yes, you are," she said. "This is an inspection. Show me around."

The sector was spotless, and working smoothly. Everyone she spoke to seemed busy and happy. At the end of the tour, she shook Fadellan's hand and promised her a promotion.

She pretended not to notice the poster of her face that had been half-ripped off the wall.

She was lounging on a *chaise longue*, eating grapes and having her feet massaged when the vidphone rang.

"Hello, Chira." Her father's face loomed down at her from the big screen, dark eyes below a mane of dark hair, streaked with grey. He took in the room, face twisting in his approximation of a smile. "I see you've made yourself at home," he rumbled.

The masseuse looked up, but Chira gestured to her to continue. "I earned this," she said. "Have you seen my numbers? Up eight percent in a fortnight."

He raised a thick eyebrow. "Impressive." He leaned in to the screen. "I've also seen your accident figures. Up fifty thousand this week. Three hundred more deaths."

She shrugged. "No matter. I increased the compensation rate. It paid for itself. And anyway, since when have you cared about the little people?"

"You can't make a profit with a broken workforce."

"Are you listening to me? Eight percent! Can any of the other four say that?"

"No, actually." He sat back, spread his arms. "I like what you've done with the place, by the way." He terminated the call.

"Nice to speak to you, too," she muttered, dropping another grape into her mouth.


There were twice as many soldiers outside the palace's grand entrance as the last time she'd ventured out. They advised her that using the back gate might be safer, but she rejected it.

"Madam President!" It was Sirren, shouting from beyond the cordon. "Madam President, you remember what you said two months ago? The permission hasn't come through yet…."

"Call the palace," she answered, not breaking stride as she and Palla climbed into the car.

"We've had a request from Sector 27," said Palla as they set off. "They're suffering a manpower shortage, and have requested any spare assets be moved to them."

"Do we have any spare assets?"

"Not really. Which reminds me: the central hospitals need more money."

"Again? No, they're just going to have to work more efficiently. And tell Sector 27 to lower the school's graduation age by two years, get people into the workforce sooner."

The Field had had an access road cut across it to the centre, where a tower, already fifty metres high, was sprouting, surrounded by hovering work platforms and machines pumping concrete up from ground level.

The crowd round the perimeter clapped dutifully as Chira got out of the car. Someone at the back shouted "Shame!" but there was a brief scuffle and the man was carried off by soldiers.

The leader of the monument project stepped forward and shook her hand. It was Galan. It was the first time she had seen him since the first night.

She leaned in towards him. "How do you like your new job?" she asked.

He smiled uncertainly. "I thank you for the honour. But—you do know I have no experience in construction?"

"That's what you pay other people for. How is the project going?"

"It's a challenging timescale you've given us. We've had to cut some corners, but we're on schedule so far."

"Good. Keep it that way." She looked up. "It's going to be magnificent."


"Strikes?" None of the fifteen senior managers around the table would meet her eye. "What's going on?" she demanded.

There was a lot of shuffling and sidelong glances. Eventually, one of the men spoke up. "You remember the

# "The Crystal Tower"

THOMAS BALDWIN is a journalist in Dunfermline, Scotland. He is married with three children, and most days commutes fifteen miles to work—by bike! "The Crystal Tower" is his first published short story.

He says: "I'd recently read *Brave New World* when I came across the Literary Taxidermy Short Story Competition. Shortly thereafter, this story arrived in my head, more-or-less fully-formed and, even more miraculously, the right length. The world of the story is obviously influenced by totalitarian regimes, but in the West we don't need to look that far for brutally-exploited workers, pointlessly-grandiose projects, and leaders who are interested only in personal glory. I'd like to dedicate this story to my grandfather, Stan Baldwin, who passed away shortly before it was written."

Steve Amos

# Thirty-four Stories

A SQUAT GREY BUILDING of only thirty-four stories.
We enter…

### 1

A couple sit at opposite ends of their sofa in the late-afternoon sunlight.

"What's pansexuality?" she asks, looking up from her magazine.

"Dunno," he mutters, eyes on the TV. "Google it."

She sighs. She doesn't want to Google it. She wants them to have a conversation. About pansexuality.

She goes over to the window and looks out on to the street. It's hard to broaden your horizons, when you're stuck in the first story.

### 2

"Boris!" cries Elspeth. "Walkies!"

Boris the cockapoo jumps from the sofa and bounds towards the front door. We're lucky, thinks Elspeth, to be on the second floor, where it's easy to get in and out of the building. She couldn't imagine having a dog if she lived higher up.

She clips on Boris' lead and they head for the park.

3

Rob is a man of regular habits: breakfast every morning at 8 am, a poo every morning at 8.30. But for several days now the poo hasn't come, and Rob's starting to feel rather bloated. He worries that he might have to see a doctor, who might find something wrong.

4

Jess cuddles Ellie in the big comfy bed. She opens her eyes and sees a shaft of sunlight coming in through the blinds. When the sunlight hits the chair, it will be time to go. Dan's making dinner, and he likes her company while he cooks.

Ellie senses that Jess is awake.

"Don't go," she says.

"Five more minutes."

Ellie loves these afternoons with Jess. She wonders if two people have ever been so happy together.

5

The couch potatoes sit in front of the TV, eating potato chips and passing judgement on the world.

"God, she's fat!"

"He's an ugly fucker!"

"Look at the ass on that!"

They watch, munch, and judge, all day long.

6

The wheels on the bus have been going round and round all day long, because Jessica just won't sleep.

"Again, mummy!" she laughs. "Again!"

So mummy sings it again, because that's what mummies have to do.

Mummy feels weary enough to sleep for a thousand years, although just ten minutes would be good. But there's no sign of that happening any time soon.

"Again mummy! Again!"

7

Dave loves rap, especially Stormzy. Like Dave, Stormzy grew up on the streets, and he tells it how it is. Dave listens to Stormzy and listens loud, but always on Beyerdynamic headphones, because they're the best you can get. Dave always uses headphones because he wants to be a good neighbor, and not everyone wants to listen to rap at three o'clock in the morning. There's a woman downstairs with a kid, for God's sake—the least he can do is allow her a decent night's sleep. You've got to show a bit of consideration in this world. Also it blocks out the noise from upstairs….

8

"Shall I call them?" asks Sam.

Jolie nods. "See if they're up for it."

Sam grins. "As I remember, they were up for pretty much anything. Especially Robbie!"

"Yeah, Gerry seemed to hold back a bit more. I'll call Robbie."

"I loved it when we were all licking each other…."

Sam looks disappointedly at the phone.

"No reply."

"Try again."

9

She hates her fucking life, in this fucking building. She tries to distract herself by reading, but it's hard, especially when the couple downstairs have people in for noisy all-night sex sessions. She puts down her book and picks up her phone. Maybe he can get her something that'll make her feel better....

## 10

"Ethelred!" cries Emma. "Will you please get ready?"

"I'll be there in a minute!"

She sighs and sits down. It always takes him ages to leave the flat.

## 11

Pete sits in front of his laptop, trousers around his ankles.

"Have you been a good boy?" asks the girl on the screen.

"Yes," he replies weakly.

"I don't think so," she says. "And I only take my panties off for good boys."

"I have been. Really...."

"*Mmm*...all right then."

She slowly pulls down her panties, all the time staring at him through her webcam. It's like she can see him, but he's glad that she can't.

"Is that nice?"

"Yes." His voice is getting squeakier and squeakier.

"Would you like me to touch myself...*here*?"

She inserts her finger into her vagina.

"Do you wish that you could touch me here?"

He swallows. "Yes."

He's masturbating hard now, as he watches her touching herself. He wonders where she lives—Russia, judging by her accent. He comes, and groans, and slams the laptop shut.

## 12

Julio's not here—not officially, anyway. He ran when he

got across the border, and the authorities have never caught up with him. He rents the apartment from the guy who lives on the twenty-sixth floor. He pays the rent by selling TV receivers, which you can use to get channels from all over the world subscription-free. He's sold quite a few to people who live in this building. He does ok. Still gets nervous when the doorbell rings, though.

### 13

She takes the pizzas from the fridge and stares at the boxes. How could she have been so stupid? She meant to buy deep pan pepperonis, but she picked up thin and crispy by mistake. Doug hates thin and crispy pizzas. There'll be hell to pay when he gets home. Her hands shake as she puts them into the oven.

### 14

Ahmed and Yohindra are fighting over the TV again. She loves Bollywood movies, but he always comes home and puts the cricket on, even when she's in the middle of watching something. It isn't fair.

When he goes to the bathroom she tunes back into her movie, then hides the remote under the couch.

She giggles. Let's see what he does now!

### 15

What do I do? I go to the liquor store, buy a few beers, then come back and watch re-runs of old football games. What's the point of life if you don't enjoy yourself, eh?

### 16

*Rub-a-dub-dub, three men in a tub.* The boys in number 16 love bath night!

## 17

Robbie scowls at the ringing phone.

"Shit! It's them!"

"Don't answer!" hisses Gerry.

"What should I do?"

"Ignore it! Otherwise they'll talk us into going down there."

"I hate those games they make us play. Don't you?"

"I didn't like being blindfolded. I couldn't tell if I was going down on you or Jolie. Can't we just stay in tonight?"

"Yeah, I'll ignore it."

"Let's open a bottle of wine and watch *Singin' in the Rain*."

"Yeah, let's do that."

Robbie's phone stops ringing. A few seconds later it starts again.

## 18

Cnut sits in his bath, trying to push back the water.

"Go back!" he cries. "Go back!"

Still the water sloshes around his buttocks.

"Tomorrow," he mutters, as he climbs out and reaches for his towel. "Tomorrow I will succeed."

## 19

There are no words for the horrors of the nineteenth story. Let's avert our eyes, and hurry on up.

## 20

His phone rings.

"Yeah?"

Silence, just the sound of breathing. He waits.

"Can you get me some stuff?"

"What do you want?"

"Something to make me feel better…."

"I need you to be specific. Skunk, hash, weed, coke, crack?"

Silence again. He can hear her thinking.

"Soma. Can you get me some soma?"

## 21

It seems weird having a sex dungeon on the twenty-first floor, but there you go. Astrid's hung heavy crimson drapes over the windows and lights the room with candles, so it creates the right ambience. Right now she's giving Anthony such a good slapping that he doesn't know where he is. He moans at the ecstatic combination of pleasure and pain, and she slaps him again with the leather strap.

## 22

Natalia sits in front of her webcam.

"Have you been a good boy?" she asks.

"Yes," he replies weakly. He's a regular, so she needs to be nice.

"I don't think so," she says. "And I only take my panties off for good boys."

"I have been. Really…"

"*Mmm*…all right then."

She slowly pulls down her pants, all the time staring at the webcam.

"Is that nice?"

"Yes." His voice is so squeaky that she almost laughs.

"Would you like me to touch myself…*here*?"

She inserts her finger into her vagina.

"Do you wish that you could touch me here?"

He pauses and swallows before answering. "Yes."

She hears him breathing faster and faster then suddenly stop, and the connection goes dead. She pulls up her pants and checks the time. Soon she'll be able to go downstairs for a glass of wine with Astrid, and hear about her day in the sex dungeon.

## 23

He stands at the window and looks wistfully out across the city. The woman he loves is thousands of miles away, with her husband. He fears that he may never see her again.

## 24

She lies on her bed with a fever, fearful that she has the virus. Her head is pounding, she can't stop coughing, and her temperature feels way over a hundred degrees. She has no energy to do anything except stare at the stain on the ceiling. She's sure it's getting bigger. When she climbed up to look, before the fever started, it felt damp, and smelled disgusting. The only good thing about this is that she's lost her sense of smell.

## 25

Mick knows that getting the dog was a bad idea, but he couldn't resist the old stray's mongrel eyes. *Love me*, they said, *and I will love you back*. He named the dog Winston.

But now Mick's old, and housebound, and can't take Winston out. Mick gets food delivered each week but doesn't order dog food, because Winston's not meant to be here. Instead he cooks him liver and kidneys and, occasionally, steak. Winston wolfs it all down, then goes to his own room to shit and piss. He's a good dog, but Mick hates to think what it must be like in there.

## 26

Gareth owns a few apartments in this building—it's like his own little empire really. There's the guy down on the twelfth floor—probably an illegal immigrant, but who cares, as long as he pays the rent. He has a different kind of arrangement with the girl in number 22—he fucks her when he wants, but by and large he just takes a percentage of her earnings. And if either of them steps out of line, he can turn them in. He's done well, got his life just how he wants it.

## 27

Dan's cooking dinner for Jess. The breeze blows in through the open window and he sings to himself, "Happy," by Pharrell Williams. She'll be home soon, and she'll sit in the kitchen to chat and have a glass of wine while he prepares the meal. He loves these evenings when it's just the two of them. He wonders if two people have ever been so happy together.

## 28

Joseph's lived quietly since Ethel died. In the mornings he puts on a collar and tie, then goes shopping. He gets a tin of soup for lunch, which he has while he watches the news. It pains him to see the state of the world, but it's important to keep up with things.

He dozes off and wakes as the afternoon sunlight creeps across the floor. He makes a cup of tea, and gets out the photograph albums. It's his favorite part of the day, looking at the pictures of their life together. Ethel was beautiful when she was young, and when he looks at the photos her smile still lights up the room. He looks back at their holidays in Crete, Corfu, and Kefalonia.

Then the music starts. Joe gets the broom and bangs on the ceiling, but it doesn't make any difference. It never does. The man upstairs stomps around singing, like he's having a party all by himself.

### 29

Nick gets in and heads straight for the record player. He's been waiting for this moment all day. He takes the seven-inch single from its sleeve, puts it on the rotating turntable, then carefully places the stylus in the groove. It crackles for a moment then starts: first the drums, then the guitars, then Mick.

Nick sings along, in full Mick Jagger mode. He struts and swaggers across the living room, wiggling his hips as he goes. He has to adapt the lyrics slightly—the "ninety-ninth floor" becomes "the twenty-ninth floor"—but it fits well enough. He's up here in splendid isolation, and you can't hang around because two's a crowd. Not on my cloud baby.

### 30

She knows what time it is, because the music starts downstairs. She knows not to schedule clients for this time, because therapy doesn't really work to a soundtrack of Sixties R&B.

Instead, she checks her email. There's one just in from someone who describes her partner as a couch potato, who just grunts when she tries to talk to him. Today she tried to prompt a response by asking him about pansexuality, but he just told her to Google it.

She sighs. What lonely lives we all lead! And the people with partners seem just as lonely as the ones who live on their own.

God, he sings loudly! She wishes he'd get off of *her* cloud. How she hates the Rolling fucking Stones.

### 31

He stands at the window and stares into the world outside. How many roads must a man walk down? And if the streets have no names, then how do you count them?

There are songs he needs to get out of his head.

## 32

"Mummy!" cries Danny. "Roland bit me!"

She sees the mark on Danny's arm.

"Roland! Did you do this?"

Roland starts crying.

"Danny was pulling my hair!"

She sighs. It's like this all day, every day.

Sometimes, when they escape from the building, she sees the young woman on the seventh floor, with her little girl. She wishes that she had girls.

## 33

Story 33 is a gym which is open to all the building's residents. Samantha sits on an exercise bike overlooking the city and pedals hard while listening to Grime. Maybe one day she'll leave the building and cycle around the streets, but not today, definitely not today. She feels panic at this thought and pedals harder to alleviate it. Samantha hasn't left this building for seven years.

## 34

We climb the fire escape to the roof and look down on the toy town city. It's like watching a colony of ants, but these sophisticated ants live in buildings, travel in vehicles, and lead individual lives. We look across the city until it fades into a distant haze. South-south-west, south, south-east, east....

# "Thirty-four Stories"

STEVE AMOS is a training consultant living in Hastings, in the UK. He tells us that his first school report said "Stephen has a good imagination, and enjoys writing long, interesting stories which are a delight to the rest of the class." So clearly not much has changed! His first book, *Two Sides of an Indie Dad*, is a mixture of fiction and autobiographical writing, published last year.

He says: "As soon as I read the opening line, I had the idea of interpreting it literally, writing thirty-four interconnected stories all set within the same building. It seemed to fit with the world of Covid-19, and the way in which our lives have suddenly narrowed, and we've become increasingly confined to the buildings in which we live."

Robert Burton Atkinson

# Mowing the Sky

A SQUAT GREY BUILDING of only thirty-four stories. This was how our insurance agent Paul Jenkins described his company's headquarters in Bloomington. Mom frowned at the word *only*, and Paul quickly explained that it was a bit of an inside joke. The original design towered to one-hundred and one stories to beat the Sears Tower up in Chicago. In the end, the company settled on a modest, and less showy, thirty-four story building, the tallest in the state south of Chicago and visible for miles in every direction.

Paul rolled his eyes as he described the "modesty" of the billion-dollar insurance company he'd represented for 30 years and again offered to drive us the two hours to the settlement meeting in Bloomington. Mom again refused; polite, but curter this time. I walked Paul to his car and promised to call if we needed anything tomorrow.

Mom and I left the next morning in Dad's truck. There's nothing much to look at that isn't soybeans or corn on the way to Bloomington, which meant Mom quickly fell asleep, chin to her chest. I'd heard her puttering around the house the night before and up early, coffee and toad-in-the-hole ready for breakfast.

I looked out at another field of soybeans. A lone, scrawny tree pushed up near its center. On the far horizon, strands of electrical lines dipped and rose between the steel skeletons so strong that they could take a direct hit from a small plane and stay standing. I thought this field might have been one of Dad's, but it's always hard to tell from the ground, and I'd stopped riding along when I was seven.

Motion sickness.

At college, whenever conversation turned to family, I didn't put on airs. Dad wasn't a pilot; he was a crop duster. Then I'd make a fart joke. If anyone romanticized it, I dispelled that notion right away by comparing crop dusting to mowing the sky. When I was little, I imagined Dad singing to himself over and over as he buzzed around the county doing sprays:

*Swoop in, do the count, swoop out, spin around—swoop in, do the count, swoop out....*

For the next field of soybeans, I counted a slow one Mississippi, two Mississippi, three Mississippi, getting to seven Mississippi at the moment Dad would have pulled the AG crop duster up and banked to clear the line of trees that ended the field. In the AG with a good start, I would've only gotten a three Mississippi count.

I was making myself sleepy estimating how many runs it would've taken to cover the field. Mom lifted her head and scanned the horizon. When the dim stain of the squat grey building finally appeared far ahead to the right of the highway, Mom pointed it out.

"That's it, I think." Mom paused, and with a low chuckle, added: "Satan's butt plug."

I almost drove off the road. "*Mom!* What the heck?"

"Blame Sam," she smiled. "He stopped by and told one of his jokes. That was one of the clean ones."

"That sounds like Sam, alright," I said, laughing. Sam owned the airfield where Dad had rented a small hanger for longer than I've been alive. Sam always both smelled of fuel and smoked more than anyone should. I once saw him grab a pesky hornet with one hand and burn it to death with a cigarette while telling Dad and I about Doolittle's raid on Tokyo. I learned how to curse from Sam. "Have you seen him much since the funeral?"

"He stops by about once a week. There's always another tool, gizmo, or whatnot that he says belonged to Dad. I told him to keep it all. It's too much. You could build another plane from all of the stuff in the out buildings that I need sort through."

The implicit task left undone and the "I" not "we" stung, though I don't think Mom meant it to.

I took the second exit into Bloomington. Dad's truck, a manual three speed on the tree, groaned as I downshifted, struggling to find second gear. Taking the truck was dumb, but it had felt so right in the moment—a last ride with Dad. But it wasn't really. He was buried at Mount Home Cemetery and the insurance company was about to pay us off.

We parked in the guest lot near the building entrance. Mom paused at a set of flagpoles outside a bank of revolving doors and looked up at the mammoth blocky grey concrete building.

"Squat? More like didley squat," I said.

Mom laughed. I'd learned about this building style in my second-year architecture class: Brutalist. I wanted to make a joke around that, but I knew Mom might not get it.

The three flags on shiny metal poles stirred in a light breeze. The white State of Illinois flag, the Stars and Stripes, and the familiar stacked circles of insurance company logo in white on a red field. Until a few months ago, that logo was peppered throughout our house on magnets, desk calendars, ballpoint pens, and various kinds of balls and baubles. After the first letters arrived, and the lawyers started calling, Mom purged it all in the burn barrel behind the garage.

"Why do they have a flag?" she asked.

"I don't know. Branding. Getting their name out there."

"They think they're a country."

"It's just a flag."

"They think they have their own laws."

A couple of passing workers glanced our way and I

gently steered Mom toward the doors. We provided our names and IDs at the registration desk and waited. I carried a leather shoulder bag with a notebook. Mom clutched her church purse tightly and watched a stream of people tap badges to open glass doors to go inside. Against the flow of bodies, a guy close to my age in a tight black suit approached and introduced himself as Kevin. We shook hands and followed him through the security door to a bank of elevators. Kevin asked about our drive in, the traffic, and parking as we rode up.

"Why do you have a flag?" Mom asked.

"Oh," Kevin looked blanked at her. "The company flag up front," Kevin said after a catching up with her train of thought. "It's our logo. All of the properties have flags. They get replaced every year on Founder's Day, which is coming up on the 19th."

"I don't care."

"Ok." Kevin stared straight ahead.

I took a chance and asked Kevin, "How's the internship program here?"

He blushed deeply as if caught, but turned to look at me. "Pretty good so far."

I needed to start thinking about starting to find internships to apply to. I wasn't a business major, but I knew plenty and some intel about this place might be appreciated.

The 17th floor office Kevin escorted us to faced south. Through a series of narrow windows, we could see a good amount of the drive we'd just taken laid out like a train model set. Mom reached over and grabbed my hand without looking at me.

The claims adjuster walked in and announced himself with short cough. "Sorry, allergies," he said.

This was Richard S. Cordry. We knew his signature. Mom had it on the letter in her purse. Our agent Paul Jenkins described him to Mom as nice, but all business. I would describe him as unremarkable. I think he would describe us the same way. We were just three unremarkable people signing legal documents, the culmination of months of paperwork, accusations, and threatened lawsuits that ended abruptly when Richard S. Cordry signed and sent a letter agreeing to pay the insurance claim in full, plus a small amount of our accrued legal fees.

Richard S. Cordry shook each of our hands and sat down.

"Thanks for coming in. There's just a few pieces of paper to sign and you can be on your way."

He spun a small stack of papers around to face Mom and set down a company branded pen, much fancier than the cheapy ballpoints our local agent had sent us every year. Richard S. Cordry explained the purpose of each document and directed my Mom to the yellow "Sign Here" tabs taped strategically throughout, which she did with her slight palsy completely under control.

Richard S. Cordry handed Mom an envelope with a check, which she folded and put into her purse without opening.

"Thank you," she said, sighing.

We stood up to leave. Kevin appeared at the door to escort us out.

"It was the compass," Richard S. Cordry said, standing up from his desk but remaining behind it. Not moving to get closer, but standing there. "The compass failed."

"What?" Mom looked up at me, to Kevin, and back to the claims adjuster.

"We investigated the crash. The NTSB missed it, but we believe the plane's compass was defective when it hit the transmission tower. Your husband's plane had defective equipment. We think that's why he crashed."

Mom snorted. "Oh, so now he wasn't drunk or negligent for going up without checking the forecast." She turned to me. "What was the other one?

"'Derelict in routine aircraft maintenance,'" I said.

"Yeah, that. Now it's the compass."

Richard S. Cordry looked down to his desk, then directly at my mother. "I'm sorry, but I wanted you to know."

Mom took a single step toward the desk and stabbed a single indignant finger downward.

"This place," she said. "This place is…never mind."

Richard S. Cordry looked down at his desk again. "I'm sorry," he said.

I moved to the door and Mom followed me out. Kevin silently led us down the elevator to the lobby.

"If you need anything," Kevin said, passing me a business card as Mom left the squat grey building without turning back.

"I'm so sorry. This has been hard on her," I said.

Kevin only nodded. I offered my hand to shake, but he was looking past me. I turned to see Mom at the flagpoles outside.

I tried hard not to run, but took long strides to meet her under the insurance company flag. She was testing the small silver padlock on the box that protected the flagpole's ropes and pulleys from the angry Moms of the world.

"So you're not the first one to try to play 'Capture the Flag,'" I said.

"We should get to the bank," she answered and walked slowly to the truck.

I glanced back to see Kevin and his suit at one of the doors, a hand up to shade his eyes against the sun's glare, which made him seem even younger to me. A boy in a man suit.

I stalled out the truck while trying to find reverse and almost rolled into a hatchback.

A few miles out of Bloomington, a slow curve of the highway put the grey squat building in the truck's rearview mirror. To the south, the towers and powerlines threaded the countryside. I still couldn't imagine Dad not seeing that tower.

"Didn't know the AG even had a compass," she said. "I thought he just, you know, looked around."

"Me too."

I didn't say anything for the rest of the drive back to our town. I let Mom out at the bank and stayed in the truck, idling in neutral with the emergency brake on. Dad's truck rumbled and wheezed in irregular intervals. I goosed the gas to keep it going a few times.

*Swoop in, do the count, swoop out, spin around—swoop in, do the count, swoop out, spin around…*

I thought about the cockpit and the gauges, levers, and switches, the flow of information and action between machine and man my Dad had mastered and I'd ignored until the compass spun wrong and brought it all crashing down.

South-south-west, south, south-east, east….

# "Mowing the Sky"

ROBERT BURTON ATKINSON is a Canadian citizen living in Maryland, in the United States. He is a content strategist by day, but also a Universal Life Church internet-ordained minister who has officiated weddings for friends—with a perfect 5-0 record. (No divorces yet!) His short story, "Skip Counting," was included in 2018's Literary Taxidermy anthology, *Telephone Me Now*. We're excited to welcome him back with another excellent story.

He says: "A certain insurance company based in central Illinois—and known for its good neighborly ways—does indeed have a large building that can be seen for miles. That immediately popped in my head, as did the idea of a spinning compass needle. Bringing those two images together were childhood memories of having our family car repeatedly sprayed by crop dusters as we drove into town. We thought it meant good luck!"

Joel McKay Pearson

# In Thunder

A SQUAT GREY BUILDING of only thirty-four stories.
On the rooftop, racks upon racks of broomsticks and a spell
to keep the rain away. The taller buildings of the wretched
boulevard climbed upward into the fog in great steps. The
shadows of witches on broomsticks criss-crossed through
the grey curling drizzle, and one shadow detached itself
from the others and drifted down to land among the aisles
of parked brooms. The thirty-four-story building was one
of many publishing houses on the east side. This one, on
levels twenty-eight through thirty-four, published the much-
respected *Howlet's Wing*: "an aspirational magazine for the
modern witch."

The shadow stowed his coat and broomstick in an area
marked *visitors* and gazed up at the domed spell protecting
the rooftop from the elements. The rain cascaded down its
sides giving him the impression he was in a colossal snow
globe. There were no stars despite it being night, though jets
of witch-fire gleamed atop some of the nearer buildings like
the flares off oil rigs. The shadow, perhaps a little nervously,
clutched a leather folder to his side and made for the
building's entrance with the air of someone with an
important appointment.

It being the witching hour, the foyer was understandably
busy with sorceresses. They made an intimidating picture to
the newcomer who was not yet accustomed to city life:
some had sieves strapped to their backs like turtle shells,
others were bearded, and one, who was trying to leave as he
was coming in, was as bald as a knuckle with a yellow beak

like a squid.

"*Mnnn,*" she growled and moved her bustled dress aside.

"Mædam," he thanked her.

"A man," she said, "there's a man here!"

The newcomer ducked into the crowd conscious that, at her age, she was sure to harbour hostility toward his sex that he could not hope to assuage even by being polite and self-effacing. Old crones remembered the old ways. But taking a verbal beating was preferable to being eyed with cannibalistic desire—another common occurrence in the city, though his evaporating youth meant he encountered it less and less.

He was relieved to see the receptionist was young and rather alluring. She was from the Boglands; he noticed a little bowl of bubbling muck at her desk with an eyedropper placed delicately over one corner. It charmed him to see it. He told her his name, Robert Chagrin, and that he was here to see the deputy editor at half past twelve.

"So you are," she agreed. "For the opening in journo." Her computer produced an ID sticker which she pressed to his chest; his heart skipped. She eyed him knowingly out of small, sideways-blinking eyes; a witch always knows what's in your heart.

"Good luck," she said. "The twenty-eighth floor. The elevator is here."

Robert was relieved to be the only one in the elevator. He pressed the button marked twenty-eight, knowing the closer he travelled toward the ground the higher the rank of witch that would be stalking the halls. The *Howlet's Wing* occupied levels twenty-eight through thirty-four, so level twenty-eight was home to the editor and deputy editor. The first floor housed the Mædam of the entire publishing house. And beyond, in the substratum of the city, the Profane Mædam held court and parliament. And some believed, deeper yet, the Unutterable Mædam turned in a womb of fire. Robert Chagrin felt so lowly having a flat on the six-hundredth floor of the complex downtown. He felt dizzy contemplating the echelons of society branching out under his feet. It was as if he were a worker ant atop an anthill, painfully aware the hierarchy always went downward, down to the queen in her holy chamber.

As the elevator sank, he checked through the folder which contained samples of his writing. Some he had cut out of newspapers and laminated—for others he had brought along the entire magazine and tagged the appropriate page. Most of his copy had to do with riding a broom and the brewing of flying ointment. Robert was a rarity among his sex—sorcery was not entirely beyond his grasp. Mixing ointment and riding a broom were things in which he was extremely adept. He pulled an article titled *Boys and Brooms* that he had written for a university newspaper as a student. It gently suggested some alterations to the ointment's ingredients to better a male's command over a broomstick. He had received a strike on his academic record for publishing it after it provoked some backlash among the students and faculty. He did not know why he had brought it. He supposed he had hoped that if the deputy editor turned out to be an open-minded sort it might very well land him the job.

Robert had spent his formative years in a little town on the edge of a wood—not the fairy-riddled sort you find in old storybooks but the plain sort; a pine plantation where the trees were kept in solemn rows. They were always felled for timber before they had a chance to grow old and gnarled. Robert thought the trees whispered their yearning to grow old to him, especially at night, for his bedroom window faced the forest. He spent much of his childhood playing there, whittling fallen boughs into wands, staves, and brooms. He felt it was important to use only wood that had fallen freely, and never wood that had been torn from a tree in a storm.

His mother, who had died nearly a decade ago, was a kind and simple witch who never had time for politics. "I have too many altars to worship at already," she used to say. She watched his yearning to wield magic and encouraged him, risking punishment from the Sisterhood for teaching a boy.

"Here, Robbie," she gave him the hawthorn bowl where she mixed her flying ointment. There was still a little salve in the bottom, leftover from coating her own broom. It was enough to coat a small broom for a small boy. "Remember to hail the quarters as you apply it." And she would sing the song of the quarters:

*Where the wind blows I go, I go. North, north-west....*

She was astounded and hugged him tightly when she saw he could make his broomstick lift its nose a little with a gesture, and tears stood in her eyes when he made its bristles twitch.

"Oh my son, my son," she said. "How is it you can do this?"

"I think it's down to your ointment, Mum," Robert said. "And perhaps the forest helped a little, too—I spend so much time there." But when at last he flew, plucking the top of his most favourite pine in the forest—the precarious one on a hill that was always forgotten by the loggers—his mother was lying silent in the town cemetery, gone the previous summer.

The wait was not long. Robert was ushered into a boardroom and deposited into an armchair that sat before an immense and elaborate desk of dark varnished wood. There was a sleek computer at its centre, various odds and ends, but most noticeably: three large bell jars that each held a contorted little creature. Each creature was different but all were long-dead, mummified, propped up on little stands. Apart from them, the desk was uninhabited.

Soon there was a click within the bookcase behind the desk. The shelves, laden with heavy tomes on publishing and marketing strategy, swung open and a witch stepped out. The deputy editor. She wasn't particularly imposing: a hunched figure, slight beneath a many-folded black robe. Her hair was lank and wet, growing thinly from her pocketed scalp. Her eyes, perfectly circular, fish-like, regarded him warily.

"Robert Chagrin, hello." Her voice wavered, at once amused and overworked. "My name is Mædam Gorja, the deputy editor." She flicked her finger and the bookshelf closed. She settled herself at her desk somewhat shakily and produced his resume out of thin air. Robert watched as the humble details of his professional and academic career etched themselves into the yellowed paper in fiery letters. She read it without looking up at him.

"Mædam…" he began, grasping his folder. He felt he would fare better if he drew her attention to some samples of his work, but she tutted him.

"Educated at Mire University. Contributed to a campus paper. Freelance from then on…. You've not written for a prolonged period for any one respectable publication, nor have you written much as a journalist, the area in which this role requires experience. And what's more, you are a male. We do not employ very many here. Given this, what makes you a good fit for this role, Mr. Chagrin?"

"That maybe, well, I've not published much journalism because I am new to the city and, well, small town papers are in small towns where nothing much happens. I have a strong record in other content, however." He opened his folder and placed a selection on her desk. He had to stand to do it for her desk was on a dais. "If you care to sample some—"

"We are looking for a journalist," Mædam Gorja said, glancing cursorily at his work. "And I will be candid, we've had an impressive run of interviews yesterday for this position. But I will keep your resume on file." His resume resolved itself into fog.

"Just a moment—" Robert blurted; Mædam Gorja had

seemed about to stand. He was still standing himself, and his tone had been unintentionally authoritative, but he saw no malice in her odd wet eyes. "Your pets," he gestured to the bell jars containing the dead things. "How did you come by them?"

"Oh, pets," she grinned, the glow of a subject that was dear to her kindling in her face. "Not quite pets. Sons. I am an unsuccessful mother, on the whole. They are dead, but I am able to commune with them sometimes." She dusted the little plaques on each: *Bartee, Beetleby, Bramblehore.* "It's the preservation spell that shrivels them so, makes them look like inhuman imps. They are growing less and less talkative as the years go by. It is an obscure spell I am still trying to master."

"What's the purpose of the spell?"

"To preserve their bodies. And to allow contact with their spirits."

"I see. A difficult spell to cast, I'm sure. Forgive my questions, Mædam," Robert bowed and seated himself.

"Don't be sorry. I display them to invite questions, do I not? I am proud of my sons. It was I who let them down. I have much sickness in my blood, in my family history. I tried to protect them from it with magic."

"I ask only because I have some knowledge of sorcery myself. Firsthand—I mean, apart from research for my writing. I am able to ride a broom."

Mædam Gorja sat up in her seat. "A rare gift for your sex."

"Not entirely a gift. I had a good teacher. My mother. I have also done a lot of experimentation—I've learnt that nightshade in flying ointment is greatly detrimental to the masculine influence over a broom. I substitute it with wintersweet. I find it multiplies my natural gifts."

"Very curious."

"I have written an article on the subject, just there."

To his surprise, Mædam Gorja read the entirety of *Boys and Brooms* with close attention. She conjured up two opalescent lenses to do so, magnifying her eyes to startling circularity.

"I do believe I use nightshade for the preservation spell on my sons," she said at last. "Perhaps that is why they come less and less. The herb has much the same function in flying ointment as it does in any spell—so I will substitute it with wintersweet." She smiled and returned Robert's stack of articles. "And...the article was constructed rather nicely. You can string a sentence or two together, Mr. Chagrin."

"Thank you, Mædam."

There was a silence as she observed him with a little admiring smile, as if daring him to ask for the job openly in light of the praise she had given him. Before the silence lingered too long, Robert, boldly with his heart hot in his throat, ventured that very question. He could hardly believe he had the nerve.

"We could certainly make some room for you here, I think," she smiled. "I will be in touch. But first, I would like to introduce someone...." She rose and bid the bookcase open once more. "It is a portal back to my home-office behind here. I will be gone a moment."

A minute past, and she returned out of the secret doorway with a boy of perhaps eight at her side. He was deathly pale and thin with Mædam Gorja's unnerving eyes. "This is another of my sons, Zadok," she said. Then bending to speak close into his ear: "This is Mr. Chagrin. Show him your secret trick."

The boy stared at Robert shyly. He had black messy hair and wore a black robe like his mother.

"Go on," his mother nudged him. "Mr. Chagrin can do similar tricks though he is a young man, like you."

The boy raised his hand and a dim fire emanated from it. The fire began small and seemed to grow to fill the entire room. The flames were gentle and colourless, making

Robert feel a little giddy as they washed through him. When the flames were swallowed back into the boy's hand, Robert saw the dead sons in the bell jars had all turned their heads to stare at their living brother.

The boy threw his face into his mother's dress to supress his smile. "Very good, very good," she patted his shoulder.

"What was the purpose of his spell?" Robert asked in wonder.

"That is your favourite refrain," Gorja laughed. "The purpose of his fire—I am unsure. The boy needs some sort of tutelage. It is not witchery. Like you, he has a sort of magic belonging to certain young men that is little understood or discussed. I think you would both benefit if some sort of arrangement could be agreed upon. Of course, I will find you a position with the magazine, but I would like it greatly if you could make time for a lesson or two a week with my son. Like his brothers, he does not often talk. It will be difficult at first."

Zadok revealed his face that still held a remnant of his hidden smile. In the boy he heard the sound of the pine forest from his childhood, smelt the sap of a newly carved broom. He felt his mother's hand on his shoulder and heard her voice call to him from the quiet cemetery where the wormwood grew.

*Where the wind blows I go, I go. Beyond the water, beyond the sea. South-south-west, south, south-east, east....*

# "In Thunder"

JOEL MCKAY PEARSON is a twenty-six year old student in Christchurch, New Zealand, and a graduate of Massey University. His short fiction "The High Road" was published in 2014 in the New Zealand literary magazine *takahe*, but this is his first success in a competition.

He says: "I had the idea for a story about witches as soon as I read the last line of *Brave New World*—it seemed to lend itself to magic. I was also influenced a lot by *Macbeth*. I hoped to explore sexism as well as motherhood in a new way, and yet keep the story light-hearted and satirical."

Damien J Howard

# Point Me in the Right Direction

A SQUAT GREY BUILDING of only thirty-four stories stood before her. It wasn't what she was promised when they moved here. When her father described it as "a concrete jungle," her imagination conjured something fun and exciting like all those weeks in scout camp out in the wilderness surrounded by trees and lakes. This was all grey and all noise. Cars honked and people shouted in languages she didn't understand.

From her bedroom window on the tenth floor she could hear it all as she looked out through the bars of the fire escape to the sheer dirty brick wall on the other side of the alley. They put a desk by the window for her to do her school work and she would spend hours peering out, searching for the beauty she had been told to expect. At night when the city lights would come on, her father would take her to the roof to show the city in all its splendour, sprawled out before her. She just felt cold, looking out at all the buildings with all the different people huddled in their boxes.

She missed the wild. She missed the trees that lined her old street, the field she would run across to get to Ben's house, the river they would run to and invent games alongside. She missed the smell of the air, the sounds of running water and the noise of animals close by.

This was a jungle of people only, built for them and them alone. And she hated it. She hated their building which looked just like all the rest. She hated her new school where kids dispersed out onto the streets to get their subways and busses home. Too far away to visit. She missed the freedom of her old home. She missed Ben.

Her father would pick her up from school every day and walk her to the subway that would take them home. Inside the apartment he would kiss her goodnight and head into work at the factory uptown, another train ride away. She would walk into the kitchen where her mother would serve her and her kid brother dinner.

That night she was greeted with a beaming smile from her mother who sat coyly at the table as they ate.

"Why are you so happy?" she asked, spooning some food into her mouth. Her brother Aldos was playing with his fork like it was a sabre and his highchair the crow's nest of a pirate ship.

"I have a surprise for you," her mother said, standing up from the table and snatching a small envelope from the counter. "You have to finish dinner before you open it." Her mother handed her the envelope and her heart started to race. She could recognise that scrawl anywhere. The letter was from Ben.

She shovelled the remainder of her food and excused herself from the table before desert was even offered and ran into her room. Sitting at her desk she ripped open the envelope and pulled out the piece of paper inside. Her eyes lit up at the string of nonsensical letters before her. Gibberish to the untrained eye, but not to her. She quickly pulled out a piece of paper and started to draw her compass.


They had made camp in a clearing beneath a canopy of tall trees that thrust up to the sky like arrowheads. The scout master pitched his tent over by the path and the others circled out from that one. The older kids helped them put their tent up to form a nice circle around what would soon become a firepit.

She was sharing a tent with Kristy, a girl her age, but she was more excited that Ben and his friend Oscar were their neighbours. Never had she lived so close to him.

With the tents pitched their camp looked like a painting of all bright neon colours contrasting against the natural rich green and browns of the forest. The scout master was gathering the older kids together and kneeling down in the middle of the camp with flint and a flat stone and a piece of wood. He was showing them how to make a flame.

She and Ben were only junior scouts—it would be a year or so before they learned how to do that—so for now they were left to entertain themselves, so long as they didn't venture too far from camp. Each of them had been given a pack with basic supplies, including her new favourite thing, a compass. She would stand still and spin in a circle and watch as the needle wobbled but kept its true north. She and Ben would play a game where they would close their eyes and spin around until they lost all sense of direction. They would then try and guess where north was—confirming it with their trusty compasses.


A year or so later back in the scout den on the outskirts of town, Ben approached her and handed her a piece of paper, on it was a short string of letters:

## E JVNI X

She looked at it confused. In school they had done Roman numerals, but she didn't recognise this as any number.

"What is it?" she asked.

"It's a code," he said with a beaming smile. "Tony showed me how to do it last night. We can use it to communicate in secret. There's a way of reordering the letters in the alphabet to a way that only we know."

"Show me!" she said excited, and he did. He pulled out a piece of paper and on it he drew a cross.

"It's like a compass," he said, pointing across the paper.

"North, south, east, and west." She nodded along. "You start at north, just like always, and you go clockwise around and list out the letters of the alphabet." He started to draw them in. "You start close to the centre and spiral out." He drew a big A at the bottom of the north axis, then a B at the bottom of the east axis, then C at south, and D at west. "Like this." He then put the E above the A on the north and kept going until all the letters were drawn out on the cross.

"Then what?" she asked, looking at the mess on the page.

"Now you have these blocks of letters for each direction. You read them outside to inside. So for north we now have..." He trailed off and she read from the page:

"Y, U, Q, M, I, E, and A."

He smiled and wrote that out for north, then the same for the other directions. "Now comes the tricky part. If you go clockwise, you write out all the letters of north, then east, then south, then west. That gives you all twenty-six letters, just out of order. You then simply replace them."

She was getting it now. "So Y becomes A?"

"Exactly." He handed her the paper and pencil. "I went clockwise."

It took her a minute to string out the new sequence of letters. To make it easier to decode, she transcribed the full alphabet in correct order underneath.

"That's called a cipher." He said, "Or something like that, anyway. It helps you crack the code. Like a spy!"

She was busy working out the code so didn't listen too intently to him. She put the letters in their places and then sat back to examine the words they made. On the paper in front of her, in her own scrawl, she read:

## I LIKE U

She started to blush. She wanted to erase the letters, to

leave it a coded message in case anyone else would see. She looked up and said "I like you" triumphantly.

"Thanks," he said back with a smile, and nudged her in her shoulder. "I like you, too."

The years passed and the letters kept coming. Each time she would happily pull the letter from the small brass box in the apartment block lobby and vanish into her room to decode the hidden message. The codes had become more complex—the same system, but they had learned how to hide their messages better.

Sometimes they would "walk the compass," and she would write something like "I'm standing at west-south-west and moving towards north." Meaning that the code would pass west first and head clockwise, so their code would be west-north-east-south.

One day she got a long letter that puzzled her. It was a block of text oddly spaced on the page. Long lines on top of weirdly short ones, sentences cut off midway and restarted on the next line. At the top of the page it read: "I have NEWS!" followed by paragraph after paragraph of rambling tales she had no interest in, about people she didn't know.

She pondered that letter for a long time, days, until she fixed on the first line. NEWS! It was an anagram for the cipher—North, East, West, South. But what was the message to decode?

Running her hand down the left margin of the page where all the sentences were aligned, she listed off the first few letters of each and began to translate using the cipher.

*There's something I need to tell you, and it's hard*, the first page read after she decoded it. She quickly moved on to the second page. She was scared to read what it could be. *We're moving away, further than you. Overseas.*

Her heart sank. Even though she hadn't seen Ben in years, there was something that made her feel that they would again. That they were connected, tethered together by a shared secret, even one as benign as a simple little code they had learned in scouts. Now he was leaving and it seemed like that tether could finally snap.

Soon, letters became emails. Ben moved with his family across the pond and he was settling in well. He had made new friends and was starting college soon. So was she, and as much as she hated to admit it to her inner child, she had grown to like the big city. She liked the pace of it. Less and less she yearned for the quiet of the country which now seemed alien to her. She now felt the grey suited her better.

Ben became her confidant, each shared message precious to her. She could write whatever she wanted, tell her deepest darkest secrets, lock them into their code where they would be safe, and send them. To write out her life in plaintext seemed too difficult—it was there for all the world to see, to be intercepted, used against her. But in code she had the freedom to say whatever she liked. Free of fear of her confessions. All the pain and heartache could be boxed away and hidden across the lines of the compass, and for one person's eyes only. And in Ben she trusted everything. He always replied, always answered her secrets with a coded reply, the unspoken understanding that to talk openly was to break some kind of vow.

One day as she sat in the college library, her makeup covering all but a hint of a bruise over her right eye, she flinched as her computer pinged with the noise of a new email. Looking up she smiled to see that it was from Ben.

He was studying English overseas and his letters read like beautiful novels where not much plot happened, but they were always a pleasure to read, with vividly drawn characters she felt she knew. They always brought a smile to her face, even when that feeling seemed so alien to her.

She found her hand shaking as she clicked to open the

letter. True to form it was long, no doubt filled with tales of his life, updates on his recent breakup and heartbreak. She skimmed it first. In her last reply to him she had buried her secret message so deep in her letter, she feared he wouldn't have found it. The thought of someone else, even Ben, reading what she had written suddenly terrified her. She had never spoken, coded or not, of what she had transmitted in her last letter.

In the middle of his long prose, in a paragraph that hung loose from the rest, he simply wrote, *I was sorry to hear your NEWS*.

There was a secret message here somewhere, a reply to hers, and she desperately wanted to read it. But it wasn't obvious. She tried all her usual tricks to find it, the first word of each line, of each paragraph. Nothing. She couldn't see where his code was.

For days she studied that letter, hiding in her living room in the dark with only the light of the screen on after everyone else had gone to bed. She even printed out a copy, hoping it might inspire her by the feel of the words on paper. "Show me," she would whisper to herself. "Point me in the right direction."

In a desperate moment she thought about writing him another email to ask him straight out where the message was. She couldn't do it, it seemed like a betrayal of the code itself. To acknowledge it was to take away all its power. If they started talking openly, she knew she would close down, she would stop. It would all be over.

Back in the library, tapping her pen furiously against the paper in front of her, the same ping noise jolted her to attention. Another mail from Ben.

She clicked it and a broad smile filled her face. It almost ached to do it, using muscles she hadn't in so long. She tore out a piece of paper and drew her compass, started to write the blocks of letters, spiralling out. She felt like the little girl in the scouts' den with butterflies in her stomach, copying out the letters of her cipher as she "walked the compass."

All the while the simple message on the screen, in three
lines, declared:

**40.7738 N 73.9708 W**
**BGGA BG VGIG WA BRKYRZVA**
**South-South-West, South-South-East, East**

# "Point Me in the Right Direction"

DAMIEN J HOWARD is an operations manager living in Dublin, Ireland. He's always had a drive to tell stories, whether it's on a page or over a drink in a pub. He is actively opposed to growing up and still gets Lego sets for Christmas. (Although he's recently discovered IKEA is Lego for adults!) He was a finalist in the Irish Imbas Celtic Mythology Short Story Competition and published in their 2018 Collection.

He says: "I've always liked puzzles, and the Literary Taxidermy Short Story Competition is a puzzle in itself. My story was born in the last line, trying to figure out how to make compass directions an important part of a story as well as a dramatic ending. In the end, I turned the puzzle into a puzzle, leaving readers with a fun little code and just enough information to figure it out for themselves."

## Anna Shannon

# The Tenant

A SQUAT GREY BUILDING of only thirty-four stories, Carol thought, wishing she could write that in the classifieds listing. *The Pomfrey* wasn't high enough to be a high-rise, but was an odd, in-between-size, in-between-era apartment, with neither modern conveniences nor vintage appeal.

She peeked out the window at what she presumed was her 1:30, Ken MacMillan. He was early for the showing, the only one booked. From the ground floor, she got a good look, squinting as she chewed on toast made from stale bread. He stood on the path in front of the main entrance and looked up, bending far backwards. Must do yoga, Carol mused. Why would he look at the roof? Nothing to see there. No, of course, he was looking up at the apartment with the FOR RENT sign on the balcony, on the top floor, above the main entrance. He took a few steps back from the door, still looking up. Finally, he planted his feet with deliberation, standing on a dandelion-festooned crack in the cement.

Carol examined his clothes: they weren't disheveled, but they weren't particularly snappy, either. He was bending over and touching—or was it petting?—a dandelion. She had given up trying to kill them. She was the super, not the caretaker. She checked: 1:28. She stuffed the rest of the toast in her mouth and, chewing hard, left the building office that was really just a desk in her bedroom, and stood in front of the mirror by the front door. As she pulled off balls of pilling from her cardigan, the intercom buzzed, and because her apartment was right next to the building's public foyer—or was it called the vestibule?—she could hear the buzzing out there too, as if in stereo.

She buzzed him into the building, then rushed out, locking her apartment door behind her. In the foyer, he was just walking in. She held out her hand, which he shook gently and for longer than she thought was standard. His hand was discoloured yellow—or was it jaundice? Yes, jaundice. Her own complexion was sallow. She'd studied her colours recently and threw out a coral sweater. Carol was an autumn. She looked up to see if his face matched his hand, and thought he might be a winter, and then looked away because he noticed her looking.

"Hi, I'm Carol. You must be Ken."

"Yes."

"Thank you for being on time." Carol removed her hand and gestured formally in the direction of the hallway. "Have you seen many apartments?"

"No. This is the only one that meets my requirements."

She led him around the corner and pressed the elevator button. The door opened promptly, and she entered briskly, turning around to stand at attention as he followed. She pressed the button with a faded three and a clear four.

"You said you're interested in *The Pomfrey* because of the view."

Carol glanced at Ken to see if he smirked when she said *The Pomfrey*. Most people smirked. She said it in a grand manner just to see if they would. Mr. Ken MacMillan did not smirk. He seemed unbothered—or maybe neutral was the right word.

"Three hundred and six feet high," he said.

"Pardon?"

"Thirty-four stories."

"That should make for a decent view, and the balconies aren't glassed-in like in the new buildings. Why have a balcony if you can't enjoy the fresh air?"

Carol hated how slowly the elevator trundled up, swaying slightly from side to side. They didn't make them this size anymore, either. Squat—or was it squalid? Squat was the right word. Wouldn't meet today's building code, but she doubted anyone would ever renovate *The Pomfrey*. On moving days, people complained they could hardly fit a double mattress in the elevator, let alone a couch. Carol felt a trickle of sweat run down her breasts and nonchalantly felt around the tendrils of her hair. She twisted them to wring them out, feeling a bit flirtatious, and steadied herself against the lurch that always came with passing floor twenty-two. She cleared her throat.

"Are you from here?"

"Does that matter?"

Carol felt shocked but looked straight ahead. He'd said it so calmly—or was it menacingly? She tried to see him with her peripheral vision. Was he looking at her? Was he clenching his fists? Maybe he was on the spectrum.

"I guess not," she said sprightly, gripping her keys, wondering if she should splay them between her fingers like she learned in self-defence class. Or maybe she had said something racist? But then they were the same ethnicity, weren't they? Maybe it was still racist.

He didn't reply, not even a polite grunt of reassurance. She breathed, not blinking, glad they were at least past floor twenty-two. Couldn't be much longer now. Finally, her body sensed a gravitational slowing. She shifted her weight from one foot to the other, ready to be the first to walk out the door, but she over-anticipated the timing and awkwardly half-stepped toward the door before it opened. When it finally did, she turned right, marched down the hall and tried to find the master key.

Carol noticed he stood behind her, not beside her, as she opened the door and braced her body to pull the key from the lock. It was stuck. She noticed there was no chivalrous offer of help, no manly shoulder thrust. She finally freed the key, banging her elbow. She recovered, stifled her irritation, and held the door open for him to pass through. She decided, from the look of his cheap haircut, that he was probably, indeed, on the spectrum; but a tenant was a tenant, and she needed a tenant. She was going to leave the door open though, she decided. He didn't say thank you, which confirmed her diagnosis. That's what people do when you open a door for them. She stood, poised, watching him enter the bathroom. She reflected, magnanimously, that she had all kinds in *The Pomfrey,* and that it wasn't her place to judge. She was their super, their superintendent, and not their superior. She shivered at the squeal of shower curtain rings scraping across metal. He came out of the bathroom with his hands behind his back, walking—or was it strolling?—on the thin-pile carpet, as if he were at a museum.

Without turning, he said, she thought pleasantly, "Looks like someone died in there."

With one eye on him walking toward the bedroom, she gripped the bathroom door and checked out the tub.

"Oh! You mean the rust stains," she said, laughing politely.

She watched him poke his head in the bedroom. He didn't go in.

"Apologies," she added. "The tub will be replaced for the next tenant."

He looked at her softly—or was it benevolently?—and said, "I'm sure it will."

Carol watched him walk up and down the galley kitchen, and tried to remember if there were any knives in the drawers. No, why would there be? Besides, he was still holding his hands behind him, hand gripping hand. No opening and shutting of drawers like others did, like kicking the tires of a car. He strolled toward the vertical blinds covering the balcony sliding window—or was it a door? She suddenly realized he wasn't about to un-grip his hands, and was waiting for her, the super, to unveil this part of the property, the part he'd been most particular about. She hurriedly opened the blinds, clicked open the lock, and with some effort, slid the window/door open.

He looked through the screen, smiling, she thought. She tried to read him, no longer caring if he noticed. He just stood there. It wasn't exactly a nice day out. It was spring and the wind was moving dark clouds this way. She shivered and took a few steps back. The wind cut through her clothes while she waited to hear what he thought. She looked around the room and took in the yellow-orange tinge where the wall met the ceiling, creating an illusion that the ceiling was higher than nine feet. She looked down. Hair had accumulated on the top of her shoes. Must be static. The hairs were short and white. Did the last tenants have an unregistered animal? Now that she was looking, it was hard to tell if they'd even vacuumed. The carpet was faintly yellow, like the walls. She sniffed the air. Did they smoke?

She stared at the back of Mr. Ken MacMillan and exhaled, then realized she should have exhaled more quietly, that he might think she sighed. He might think she's rushing him. She needed a new tenant for that bonus. Not like she could spend it anyway. Just going right on the credit card. The things we do for money, she thought. Her toes pinched. She hadn't planned on being the super for this long. She had plans, and she wasn't bad looking. She just needed freshening up, like the apartment. Carol felt a gas bubble move in her abdomen. The dim light from the balcony was making her tired. She was getting cold. How long was he going to stand there? He wanted a view. This was a view. If he wasn't going to go on the balcony, he could at least close the window/door. Maybe he expected her to do that, too. Burping silently, she walked towards him, still keeping a few feet apart.

He un-gripped his hands and rubbed them on the side of his pants. She looked at his knuckles, a man's knuckles. Yes, she needed to make some changes. Get a new job. Get a man. Get a makeover. The stupid bonus wasn't worth living in this shit-hole building, showing units to creeps. He could kill her right now and no one would notice she was missing, not until the first of the month anyway. That was almost two weeks away. But why would he kill her? She hadn't done anything to deserve it—but then what did that matter anymore? The world was going to shit.

"May I?" Carol asked, as she slid the screen open, wondering if he had a disability—no it was *lived* with a disability, and not *had*. Maybe he had something wrong with his hands.

He stepped onto the balcony. Like the elevator, it was small, squat. Just big enough to comfortably hold him and two abandoned chairs. He turned around to face her.

"This will do just fine," he said.

Carol couldn't read his expression, shadowed against a sudden light through parted clouds.

"I'll take it. Today."

"Awesome! I mean, I'm delighted to hear that Mr. MacMillan."

"Oh, please, call me Ken. Mr. MacMillan is my father's name."

He laughed, and she laughed politely, then she laughed heartily to match his laughing.

"I guess I should get the paperwork. I'll be back in a jiffy, Ken."

He stepped back into the living room and she closed the screen and window/door. She felt relief to see he was smiling—no, grinning—widely. His eyes seemed oddly blue, but maybe it was the odd light. It made his skin seem shiny—or waxy.

She exhaled, and her shoulders relaxed. There was nothing to worry about. This was Ken: Ken who made lame jokes, Ken who liked a view.

"So can I just ask, what kind of view do you need?"

"Southerly."

Carol looked at the landmarks outside, at buildings even more squat than *The Pomfrey.*

"I think this is more south-west, no, wait, south-east. It's been a long time since Girl Guides."

She laughed, indulging herself. After all, Ken laughed at his own jokes, too.

But then he began to snap his fingers in what she felt was an alarmingly jolly rhythm. He closed his eyes and began to sing:

"*South-south-west, south south-east, east, bom bom bom, my baby likes the east the least.*"

Carol closed her mouth and felt the gas shift inside again. She preferred the quiet, brooding Ken to this, whatever this was.

"Think I'll make the charts?" he asked, laughing at himself. "Good thing no one will hear me from the thirty-fourth floor."

"True enough," said Carol. "Ok, Ken, back in a jiffy."

She wondered why she'd said that. She never said jiffy.

"Thanks again, Carol. I appreciate it."

He held out his hand and she shook it, thinking it was too soon for the handshake. That was for after he signed the paperwork. That was just like Ken.

"My pleasure," she said.

As Carol left the unit, she heard the balcony window/door slide open again, and felt a breeze push through the hall. She hummed, all the way down the elevator, all the way into her office, where she realized she was humming his made-up song, and then she thought, to hell with it, she was getting that bonus. After this she'd get a bottle of wine and a piece of carrot cake from the grocery store, and rent a movie maybe. As she printed off the forms, she found herself singing:

"*South-south-west, south south-east, east, bom bom bom, my baby likes the east the least."*

She felt good, silly even. Maybe this was the start of something better. Maybe this summer she'd get out of debt, take that spin class, meet someone. Maybe there were possibilities with Ken, even. He wasn't that bad-looking. A little weird, but then wasn't she just as weird, singing a song he had just made up.

She snatched up her keys, and only paused briefly in her singing, hearing a muffled thump outside her office, outside the building, near the main entrance. Probably a package being dropped off, dumped unceremoniously as usual. She closed the apartment door behind her, and jauntily walked toward the elevator, glancing outside the main entrance, singing:

*"South-south-west, south south-east, east—"*

# "The Tenant"

ANNA SHANNON is a writer in Calgary, Canada. As a child, she read every novel she could get her hands on—which turned out to be mostly Victorian gothics. This is one reason she'd recite Tennyson in her backyard against raging thunderstorms, or read Poe by candle-light to distract herself from the swaying of a high-rise during a typhoon. "The Tenant" is her first published short story.

She says: "We are all made of bits blown apart and clumsily put back together, and life is never as it seems. Perhaps this is why I find literary taxidermy so enthralling. Years ago, while volunteering at a suicide call centre, someone told me about a suicide by a darkly clever man who selected an apartment for rent at the top of a high-rise. I've never been able to get that scenario out of my mind and, faced with the description of a 'squat building,' I thrilled at the chance to include it in this piece."

Helen J Firminger

# The Grey Hut

A SQUAT GREY BUILDING of only thirty-four stories. Tales painted or scratched on leather or stone. It lurked in a hollow in the damp woods. It was not on any path, yet it ended up on mine.

I fell, slipping on the muddy slope, clutching at the stalks of late summer irises, sliding through the wet brambles, into the cattle-grazed clearing. I hauled my damaged leg and sweating weary body to the low entrance, too low for the cattle. From inside a face like an egg looked out. Alana the keeper—beautiful, terrifying, and ugly.

We sat in the small dark space, with our toes touching, my satchel by my side, while Alana sparked a light. I caught my breath. The wall to one side of her head held the first set of stories. I scanned these slowly: a tale of a dear friend lost at sea; a pregnant figure with many children; a storm caller, giving rain to her people; a healer of ills, who could not heal herself; an overlong saga of a sword-wielder and their battles; a woman who waited at the window and what she saw; a castle builder and how she bought the secret of keeping back the sea; a gardener nurturing a flower through a drought in hope for the tiny seeds.

Alana patiently held the light for me to read and imagine. Some of the stories were on fabric, or wood; others etched on round stones. I turned my neck, there were more. The low room was built with walls like a five sided coin, each side covered in stories. They were written in different hands, different letters, different languages. Some were pictures. Each in their place. There was a low bubbling stream and a black mirror in the middle. It felt like a puzzle.

"This is the house of thirty-four stories," Alana whispered, her dark face too close to mine. "There are four walls, each with eight stories—"

"Out there," I interrupted, pointing quickly through the doorway, across the crook branch of the oak and the birch and blackberries opposite. "If this wood were to kindly move aside, you would see the mountain where my people are; that way, into the sun. Our house, my mother, my sister, our dogs…." I faltered, then began again: "You would find the path down through the trees easily, it is not far from here—that way," I pointed again. I felt trapped by the stories, and the trickling stream. I did not want to know the answer to the puzzle. "There is a hollow by the stream with lace flowers, you can camp there, then cross the river at first light in the secret place, I could show you." I was urgent now, though I had no idea for what I was bargaining. I held her eyes a while then let the breath go to the side. "Or you could take the road and cross at the toll bridge at the town they call Roses, it is further, but you could do that." I picked at the mud on my good knee.

Alana began again. Her skin looked very smooth and old in the low light.

"Every two years, someone comes, a woman. She tells her tale. She drinks from the well. She stares into the mirror, and she leaves her story here."

"How do you live here, what do you eat?"

"There are places in the woods, the villagers and herdsmen remember, they leave me food and milk. Would you like some sour cabbage? Some dry apples?" She waved gracefully at several covered bowls.

I shook my head and reached to the wall to touch a round stone. I traced the design with my fingers. Two women, one man. An old story. "I could take you anywhere," I said. I pulled the stone from the wall and held it tight. "I am a wayfinder. I can take you anywhere. We could go the other way, through the canyons to the coast. There is a port at Lee, we could take a boat out to where the snow wind comes from. It is more dangerous, in the hills that way, there are bad men who walk with knives and traps, but I know the paths. They haven't caught me." Alana looked politely at my injured leg. "They haven't caught me," I repeated.

Alana began again:

"Every two years, a woman comes, she drinks from the well, she looks in the mirror, she leaves her story, and then she dies."

I gripped the stone again, there was gold highlighting on the dresses. I raised my chin proudly to say the words clearly: "My people call me the wandering dog. In our language we have many different words for what you call dogs. We have words for cartdogs, sheepdogs, cattledogs, female dogs in heat, fighter dogs, little suckling puppies, mother dogs, dogs that work the well machinery, and dogs that keep old blind grandmas safe. We only have one sort of dog, but so many words it is hard to talk about dogs in any other language." I realised then that I did not know in which language we were talking.

Alana had the cup in her hand now, she had filled it from the bubbling upwell. There was a smell, something that caught at the back of my nose, a tang like cleaning metal with vinegar. I remembered taking rust from my icehooks in springtime with the little white flowers at my feet. It gave me some courage.

"This cannot be the house of thirty-four stories. There is the door and there are four walls each with eight stories. That is not right. The numbers do not add up. The door is not a story."

Alana drained the cup, droplets running down her arm to stream off her elbow.

She leant forwards to gaze into the mirror. It was a dark glass that went down a long way. She stared for some time.

I thought of faraway hills and the route to the river source and a place where good chicken mushrooms grow. I had not been that way for many years, perhaps I would go home that way.

"To the left of the door is an alcove that is awaiting my story. It is my time now." Alana raised her eyes, they seemed silver. I thought maybe they had always been silver. The rain had stopped and it was dark outside. She leant back and began to scratch her story with a knife into a piece of light birchwood. She scratched deep and long, so the tale would last. I could see those clever silvering eyes. I waited, holding it in. She held up the wood, and placed it in the niche.

I read her story:

$$2 \times 2 \times 2 \times 2 \times 2 + 2$$

I did not want to ask because I did not want to hear the answer. I did not want to ask because the mountain path was calling. "I am fit and strong," I called, too loudly in the tiny hut. "I can carry you over the mountains." I flexed my arms. Alana's silver eyes looked at the wrinkled skin over my tight muscles, the crossed scars, the brown spots; they travelled down to my leg where the shin bone was jutting slightly, glistening in the rushlight. I did not want to ask.

"Whose story is the last one?"

Alana had pulled herself through the doorway into the quiet night. The eyes looked back at me now, shining with moonlight. They held mine as her breath became shallow.

As the morning sun rose, I made ready a paste of paprika and oil, mixing it with a fine stick, and cut the leather piece from my old satchel. I took the cup and drank the bitter well liquid. I gazed deep and long into the mirror and saw the high passes around my home, the sheltered caves and secret springs which sustain my people, the inner needle we hold which takes us back there without maps wherever you may put us. I saw the wind high on the cliffs of the peak we call the watchtower, the spring bears fishing in the long waterfall, the little white flowers among the rocks.

I took my paste and wrote the directions slowly and inevitably:

*South-south-west, south, south-east, east....*

# "The Grey Hut"

HELEN J FIRMINGER is a parks officer living in London, in the UK. She love maps and walking so much that she thinks she writes with her feet. "The Grey Hut" is her first published short story.

She says: "It was the compass points started it. So I went for a walk in the woods up the hill, and when I came back I had my rangy aging guide who knows every road and secret path. She is called Tarka. Then I started at the other end with the stories and walked among the trees, and there was Alana waiting among the oaks. Alana and Tarka had a chat and we worked the story out together. I couldn't have done it without them."

# Cornucopia

A SQUAT GREY BUILDING of only thirty-four stories
was a roundabout to them. Burra caught a branch leaning
through a window, and swung past the vines that twisted
across its façade. It had cost Burra an arm and a leg to have
a daughter. It had cost him his other leg to raise her. She
was not a weight to him, though, and he carried her lightly
on his shoulders, balanced with his real hand on her ankle.

"Here comes another one, Daddy!"

The both ducked as a shit monkey leapt up past them,
trowel held in the tail curving over its back. The monkey
rushed, spitting and yowling, raising a cluster of pigeons into
the morning's bright heat, and busied itself scooping guano
into the panniers on its back. Burra moved his claw to steady
Mally, and raised his hand over her head to shelter her from
the little rain of shit.

Sheltering Mally had been his life for the past five years.
Birds and monkeys were a small annoyance; the biggest
danger was other humans. The exploitation of willing flesh
was not enough for some; they craved pain and humiliation.
He re-tuned his grip, feeling the curve of her foot safe in his
hand.

"Watch it! Coming down now!" The monkey brought a
small landslide of leaves onto the ruptured cobble of the
street. It bounced through the curve of Burra's running
hooks and dashed away.

In the old days, he'd raced monkeys. It wasn't legal, but

if you paid a man enough.... They were more agile than a human, but they lacked stamina and were poor performers in water. He'd done eight and ten hour chases through the trees and towers and tanks of the city. He'd run and swung and bounced and clung and swum and leapt and hung until he thought that his tsunami heart would shatter its cage, his cyclone breath would shred his lungs, his earthquake muscles would pull him all apart; then he would stand on the winner's podium, creating a whole new microclimate as the heat boiled off him and the sweat rained around him; and he would feel the sun and the earth and the stars and the moon and glory in being connected to them all.

He was not good enough, though. He was never going to earn his way out of the city; he would have to buy it.

Mally's fingers clutched his hair. "Can I have ice cream, Daddy?"

Little costs. A thousand scars.

He paid with hair and blood. One last treat for Mally that he allowed himself to enjoy as well. The thrill of cold coconut crystals melted on his tongue. The sweetness of berry syrup was counterpoint to the feelings that he swallowed. Mally was his. She had cost him three limbs and this next meeting would cost him the fourth, but his life was going to change. No more vigilance against freelancing shit monkeys or follicle thieves and vamps, waiting to steal away every shed hair and spilled drop of sweat.

"Daddy?"

"Yes?"

"Run fast."

"You'll drop ice cream on my head."

"No, I won't. Run fast."

His hooks flexed and he raced; long, loping bounces as easy as moonwalking. He ran through the city with the warm wind in his hair, felt the slight tug and give as she grabbed the ends of trailing vines, heard her call out to friends. There was Lek, lolling on a tree-branch, weaving hair and beads and brilliant feathers from her slub lorikeet. Fino, grinning as he lugged water to his bath house.

"Are they going to chop off my legs when I grow up?"

"You're not going to grow up, Mally. You'll always be a little girl."

"Look. It's raining rainbows."

Shredded leaves and petals fell about his face. He laughed.

They were coming up hard on the gateway. The guard drew around him like a fist.

"Come on, Daddy." Mally knocked him with her feet so that he bounced a little. "Don't stop."

"I have to."

"But why?"

"The guard has to make sure that we're allowed to go on."

"Well, tell it. Tell it we can. Tell it I want to run."

"I am telling it."

Iris scan, mouth swab, random flesh analysis. A thousand little scars. Everything had a cost. His right arm hung like a pendulum. The guard whispered an affirmation.

Beyond the jungle barrier of the city was the wonder and the majesty and differentness of metropolis. In his mind, he echoed Mally's awe-struck _aaah!_ as they raced along the smooth paving of hard, white road. Here were buildings so vast and solid that they cast shadows over the trees. There were no vines twining through windows. There were no drifts of rotting leaves. He saw people in humming vehicles, their bodies draped and covered.

"Daddy, they've got clothes."

"Yeah."

"You can't even see their arms and legs."

"It's not just their bums that are covered, is it?"

"Have they got arms and legs?"

"Of course they do," he said.

"But some of them might have wheels. This is a good road for wheels."

He was surprised by the intelligence of her observation. She'd always surprised him. From the moment when she'd first been given to him, still curled and hot from her mother's body, she'd had the ability to show him that there were perspectives he'd never thought of.

That was why he'd bought her. He reminded himself as his hooks whipped and sang, she was there so that he could have a different life. Cold air spilled from open doorways, and behind façades made of solid glass he could see the bright shine of things that were fresh-milled and clean.

"This is a very special place, isn't it?"

"This is the metropolis."

"How long do we have to stay here?"

"This is our home, now."

"But there aren't any vines here, or birds."

"Well there also aren't any monkeys that come to steal your shit, and inside the houses it's clean and dry."

Burra stopped at the door of a building with a façade that glimmered like moonlight on water. Transponders introduced him and the door opened.

It was cool. "You can hop down now." He lifted Mally from his shoulders but kept her hand in his. They walked side by side through a vast atrium with murals of flowers and trees and birds and insects, each one perfect and none of them any real thing that Burra had ever seen. A door opened and they stepped into a tiny room.

Burra whispered, "This room can move."

Mally's hand tightened and her eyes went wide as the lift carried them up. "This is like flying."

They arrived at Ranken's house. There were soft cushions that Burra wanted to touch, but he knew he would leave a mark, thick and dirty.

Ranken was exactly as Burra remembered from five years ago: a slender man with dark eyes and sleek, cropped hair. He wore pants that covered all the way down his legs, a shirt with fastenings at the front, and sleeves that went to his wrists. Burra wondered what it was like, all that cloth surrounding his body.

Ranken greeted him with extended hands.

Burra clasped his fingers and it was only after he had kissed Ranken's knuckles in the formal way, and was seeing the smudge of Ranken's exhalation against his claw, that he realised he had let go of Mally's hand. She was in Ranken's house now. She belonged to him.

"The deeds then," Ranken said. "Let's get this all over."

Burra took the deed from the carrysafe in the connecting rod between his claw and elbow. His stomach twisted and knotted in fear, and it embarrassed him that he could feel doubt. He knew all was in order.

Mally climbed onto Ranken's chairs as if she was on the big, solid branches of their tree. She was not vat-incubated or a slub imprinted with synthetic DNA. He'd chosen the finest breeder he could afford, and had gene weavers put together the best zygote. He trusted in the health, strength, intelligence, adaptability, and endurance of his daughter.

"You should see this, Daddy," her face pressed to the window. "It's like the box, only we're inside, looking out."

"Nice mix." Ranken glanced up from the data feed. "She looks good, too."

"She's perfect."

Ranken pointed at the deed. "Even these can be faked."

"Maybe." Burra nodded towards Mally. "That can't, though." He'd breastfed her himself. There was always fresh fruit, clean water, abundant vegetables, and he'd fed her protein every single day of her life. He'd seen poor little slubs whose only purpose was to placate the maternal requirements of some feral unfit to breed, their dull eyes and slow wits a foretaste of an eventual fate as servants or sex slaves. He thought of Mally's joy and enthusiasm, her teeth cracking through the carapace of a cockroach, licking the pale cream from its shell, of her by the fire, holding a stick with a big spider spitted on it, hardly able to wait, wanting to eat it before it was done crispy with all the hairs singed off its legs.

"Yeah," Ranken said. "She's good."

There was a hard weight in Burra's stomach. Since the moment he'd fisted himself into a jar and given it to the gene weaver, this had been all about buying his freedom. And this was her escape as well. Whatever it was her new owners did, it had to be better than gathering her own excrement to trade for food, or weaving the dull feathers of a slub parrot.

She had her back to him, the golden-ginger of her hair haloed in brightness, hands pressed up against the glass, head tipped back, staring up at clouds that floated in a sky as blue as her eyes. He left without saying anything.


Burra's wounds healed and the scars itched and tugged at the base of his new arm. His body was light and fast and balanced now. His skin was as clean as the sheets he slept on. His world was cool and empty. He wanted to invite birds and animals into his house. He wanted Mally. He had Ranken's invitation to society.

Amberly was the owner of the best team in the world, and Burra had been invited to his daughter's thirteenth birthday. He'd bought a suit of shining grey with pants that covered his legs to the ankle-curve of his hooks and a shirt that had sleeves down to his claws. He wore underwear; the tightness of it around his middle reminded him of his old chasing strip, but it held his cock like a comfortable sling so that he didn't feel that peculiar vulnerability he got from not having thighs.

This was Amberly's daughter's formal introduction to society. Burra brought the gift of a snake circlet that reminded him of the snake from his house in the city. The other guests wore suits—black and blue, shimmering gold, pink, and grey—just like his. He fitted in. They carried gifts and some were bigger than his, and some were smaller.

The women draped their bodies with fabric that clung to their thighs and breasts so that it made him wonder if they really had the same bodies as the women of the city, or if there was something special under there. They shimmered like lizards in the sun, like the wings of dragonflies.

Burra helped himself to a blue drink and followed the guide signal to Ranken. There were other team owners here; he would be introduced to all of them.

Servants carried plates of food: toasted cashews and deep fried locusts, honey cakes and cantaloupe, lychees and creamy widgedi grubs, grapes, and pistachios. One day this might be Mally. He took a pink drink. This was how box people lived.

He swayed and lurched on his blades, the world had become unsteady. "Here." Ranken eased him onto a seat. "Should have warned you about those pink drinks."

A white stage lifted Amberly and his daughter. She was blonde and pale, wearing a rainbow dress that danced in tatters and ribbons of colour. Burra felt a sudden, terrible pain in his balls and his guts and his head and his heart because this was Mally as he would never see her.

"Is this real?" he said.

There was this flat plane of grass, so green and smooth that Burra wanted to roll naked on it. It erupted into a dance of tiny flowers that reflected the rainbow colours of the girl's dress.

On Mally's birthdays, they'd sat under the big leaves of the ice cream shop with Lek and Fino and told jokes and stories. He'd carried her on his shoulders around the whole city, leaping across balconies and racing along walls, splashing through water tanks.

"Oh, there's more," Ranken said. "Thirteen. Year of change. She wanted a unicorn."

"Unicorn?"

"*Shh*. Supposed to be a secret."

Bootstrap geneweaving. Pathetic slub chimeras patchworked together. Dragons that breathed fire once or twice until their lungs burst and they immolated. Would this just be a deformed horse? He was disappointed. Slubs were playthings of fuck addicts and gruehounds and lonely ferals. They lacked dignity. "Why would a kid want that?"

Ranken shook his head and then put his mouth to Burra's ear. "They got live matrix."

"Filthy!" Shock and fury erupted out of him and he wanted to hurl the half-full glass of pink drink at Amberly. What animal had been broken and peeled and tortured so that a child who didn't care could have a pet that didn't matter?

"*Shh!*" Ranken waved down Burra's outrage. "They used *human* matrix," he raised a finger. "Legal procurement, my friend."

The crowd surged as the platform grew a second tier. Doors opened and the unicorn stepped out.

Its horn reflected nacre-rainbows, a shimmering pearl of an animal.

It saw Burra, and tossing its golden-ginger mane, leaped from the stage. It snorted and pawed the ground and the crowd drew back, a little afraid. It gazed up at Burra, eyes blue as Mally's. He smoothed its neck with the curve of his claw. The people drew in and Amberly's daughter squalled with rage. The unicorn nodded at Burra.

He got up, unsteady on his hooks. The people pulled aside. Burra tore his shirt and pants away, the sun turned him to gold. He could feel the stars and the jungle and the unicorn and he had the glorious knowledge that he was connected to them all. He turned and with the unicorn ran—towards some distant freedom, bouncing crookedly across rainbow-flower meadows, south-south-west, south, south-east, east....

# "Cornucopia"

AMANDA LA BAS DE PLUMETOT says she is "just a lady who sells popcorn in a cinema" in Melbourne, Australia. But we think she underestimates her success as a writer. Her work can be found in *Best Australian Stories 2006* and the short-story collection *Briefs*. Her story for this year's literary taxidermy competition offers a unique take on Huxley's first and last lines. The alien world she conjures is simultaneously primitive, futuristic, and surreal; and we loved the Joycean quality of her language. The story was a thrill to read and a pleasure to award.

She says: "I'm a granny that works in a cinema so I've had a lot of spare time during lockdown. During a recent writing camp I wondered 'what do monsters do with the children they steal?' My friends thought the answer was obvious: sexual enslavement or cannibalism. But I thought there might be a different possibility…."

# Sharp Edges

A SQUAT GREY BUILDING of only thirty-four stories was all it took for Lance to die. I didn't scream when he jumped.

My whole life, I followed that boy around. Behind the rough mask of delinquent-kid with no mum and a drunk dad, he was technicolour, intoxicating, intense. He had a tall, svelte frame, built for strength and high velocity. Eyes the shade of winter blue that made you think of crisp water and icy breezes. Dark, ruffled hair that cracked with static and smelled like wood and hay. Gentle hands that could punch through wall and bone, but also caress, hold, embrace. He was built for life. He was life. Far too three-dimensional to find his demise in such a flat and unassuming place.

I will never truly understand how plain, shy, mousy little me ended up with him. We were young when we first met. I was ten, he was fifteen, and I was annoying. He would hurl abuse at me as I shadowed him wherever he went, hopeful and eager. His eyes would fall on me, ablaze with contempt and beautiful on the backdrop of sky. He tried his best to shake me off. He would peg pebbles at my head and sprint away as fast as he could. But I was relentless. No matter what he did, I was right there behind him, beating my tiny legs as fast as they could go, head bruised and bleeding, tears of pain stinging my eyes. He could do nothing to deter me. Life with Lance was thrilling. Before he came into my world, I was sure this must be hell, sure that life could not be this dull, stale and...lifeless. His electricity jumpstarted my soul and brought me into sharp focus. I was addicted. He would say to me later, *Sadie, I could never be rid of you even if I wanted, you're too strong for me*, and I would laugh because he was the sun and I was just in his orbit, feeding off his light.

We were platonic, at first, and an unlikely pair. I was still skinny and awkward and flat as a rake. My features were too big for my scrawny face, and I wasn't old enough for my freckles to be cute, yet. He would put me on lookout during his many missions, and I would dutifully, desperately, keep him safe. Or so I thought. Most "missions" ended with him in handcuffs and my father in a fit of fury. I don't know why we did half the things we did, but when that boy got an idea in his head, he was convinced it had to be done, life or death. I never questioned, I simply followed, life or death.

Many years later, things changed. I was taller, still plain, but prettier, softer, curves of femininity starting to take form. He had gotten used to me as his shadow. We were trekking through the forest once, one of his grand adventures, and he got us lost. I could see he was walking us in the wrong direction, but I was enjoying too much the feeling of being tugged along in his wake to say anything. "We have to head west," he said, pointing to the south. He was beautiful; buzzing and breathing with the forest around him as I tentatively reached out and moved his hand. "West" was all I replied. I had never corrected him before, never offered a suggestion, or spoke other than to respond. His eyes penetrated mine, assessing, calculating. Without a word, he set off in the direction I had set, his legs angry and defiant. It was a tense walk. He was gripped with danger and curiosity as we trudged through seemingly never-ending trees. At the first sign of streetlights he rounded on me. I couldn't see his eyes clearly, but I felt them keen on my soul. Under the moonlight I could see his pulse thrumming under his skin and feel mine throbbing in its rhythm. He grabbed my head and kissed me hard. We were different after that.

*My compass*, he would call me from then on. I wish I could describe the ecstasy of being invited into such an exotic universe, and able to influence such a potent force. *Left or right?* he would yell over the sound of his engine whining from the astonishing speed. Left. *Stay or leav*e? he asked when we had stood on my front lawn, gazing at each other, my father screaming at me to get inside. Leave. *Palm or knuckles?* he would growl. In those moments, I would remember what he always told me: *life should be felt, Sadie, why would God give us pleasure and pain if not to find its edges?* I would always choose knuckles.

The few people around me I had left would ask, *why do you stay?* I never bothered answering because I knew they could never understand what it was to live life with utter conviction, to explore the full range of experience. Lance taught me to live in extremes, to live with sharp edges. *I'm lost!* he would wail. *You're found,* I would say, squeezing him until he oriented himself again. *I hate you,* he would scream, with such venom. *I love you,* I would reply, with such tenderness. *Life is a seesaw,* he said, *stand in the middle and what's the point?* You cannot have love without hate, nor pleasure without pain. He taught me that.

Even in our darkest moments, he remained impassioned. When we moved to the city, living in an abandoned knitting mill, and I was shivering and exhausted from the elements, he would tell me, "Sadie, my love, inside everyone is a peasant and a king. If everyone realised that, the world would have no problems. When a man is feeling like a peasant, he feels sorry for himself and cannot see beyond his small world, so he stays a peasant. He doesn't realise he is also a king. Another peasant works hard and makes himself a king with his very own kingdom. He'll fight to stay a king. He will lie, cheat and steal to keep his crown and all he has conquered. He is blinded by ever greater horizons, and he forgets he is also a humble peasant. If everyone would take their turn playing their parts in life, the world would turn as it should." Although I didn't always grasp the things he said, they always brought me comfort. He said them with such force, I was swept away in the torrent of his power and they became my thoughts, too.

I have to admit, I silently worried for him as more years went by. He spoke lengthily of quantum physics, other dimensions, other worlds, and many strange concepts I couldn't wrap my head around. He would rant hungrily about how nothing is real, that we are nothing but a dream, a hologram, a wisp of some giant imagination. He was convinced that with the force of his mind he could bend reality and defy the laws of our physical world. His blue eyes would stare greedily into things I could not see, his ears would welcome whispers I could not hear. He was going to do it, he decided. He was convinced. He crackled with electricity and I could think of no force in the universe that could possibly defy him. So, like always, I was convinced, too.

*Take me, my compass,* he had said, wanting me to choose the place where he would challenge God himself. I navigated us through the city in search of the perfect spot. *West, north-west, north, north-north-east,* I would whisper to myself, committing our path to memory so we could find our way back through the vicious concrete maze. *Compass of my heart, navigator of my soul!* he had laughed, maniacally, as he enveloped me with warmth and safety. I twisted my doubts into enthusiasm and settled into his joy. It soon faded.

There was a violent wind that day, coming from the east. It tore at my skin and my hair whipped at my face unforgivingly. My eyes stung as I kept them locked on Lance standing precariously on the edge as the wind threatened to knock him off before he could jump. The sky was as grey as the ledge he was perched on, making the world seem opaque and two-dimensional, as if he were merely standing before a solid grey wall. He turned to look at me, blue eyes alight, lips moving frenetically, but all I could hear were my eardrums shuddering and pounding. Then he leapt.

I didn't scream.

I didn't scream because for a second, I actually thought he had succeeded in defying the Almighty. His feet left the ledge, his body was spread-eagled against the flat backdrop of sky that made him look unreal, like a figure in a cartoon. He flung to the left and for that short pinprick in time my whole body jolted and my heart swelled into my throat because I actually thought he had done it. I actually thought he was flying.

Then he dropped mercilessly. Apparently, we are prisoners to the laws of our universe, and it is a prison we cannot easily escape. Gravity was the warden on duty that day. He was home to God before I could let out a sound.

Sometimes I lay in bed at night and I tell him why I didn't scream, that I love him and hate him at the same time. Knowing Lance, he will be listening from some other plane, calling me a silly girl, whispering that we exist in all dimensions at once, and that I just have to reach out and touch him. But I don't know how to live in all dimensions at once. I only know how to live in this one. I don't know how to break the laws of the Universe, so I am stuck in this prison until God decides that I have served my time, that I am finished being punished for whatever it was that I did before I came to this strange place. This weird hell where you can't have pleasure without pain, or love without hate.

When my edges become hazy and my breath halts in my throat, I find myself on the ledge of that dull and unassuming place. I look down to the pavement below and imagine him in all his colour. I drink in the vision, vivid red filling my world. I think about joining him, wherever he is. The muscles in my legs ready themselves to jump at the thought. Even in death, my body still follows him blindly. The impulse to leap is enough for me to feel my edges again. Life should be felt, he taught me.

Feeling fragile and sharp, I hop down from the ledge and carry myself away. I wonder what laws govern the world he inhabits now. I wonder if he is lost or found.

In case he still needs a compass for his heart and a navigator for his soul, I whisper aloud, *south-south-west, south, south-east, east.*

# "Sharp Edges"

LOLLY ALDER is a former Pilates instructor, living in Melbourne, Australia. She dearly hopes to be a *future* Pilates instructor, too, once we're through the present Covid-19 pandemic. Some of her favorite things include watermelon, waking up comfy and having nowhere to be, and searching for the perfect word and finding it. "Sharp Edges" is her first published short story.

She says: "I was reaching into all sorts of strange worlds for inspiration and started two stories that fizzled before they could finish. The melancholy 'grey' of the squat building and the sentimental and lonely tones in the last line reminded me of a short piece I had written years ago and forgotten about. It seemed what I needed was right under my nose, and with the fresh injection of energy from the Huxley lines, I reworked it—and voila!"

Josephine Greenland

# Compass of the Winds

A SQUAT GREY BUILDING of only thirty-four stories. Dark slits no wider than a sewing machine for windows. It rises above the tenement flats, staring down at the whizzing traffic as if confused about how it got here. It does not have a door, but two armed guards watching the entrance. A passage the width of a car leads the way into a dim-lit mall crowded with t-shirt shops and market stalls. There is no way around; to reach the stairs at the other side which lead past the office spaces up to the factory floors, one must weave one's way past the stalls, bumping shoulders with vendors, buyers, and workers hurrying to pick up a packet of biscuits or a *bhel puri* before their shift starts.

But today the mall is empty. So too the offices on the first three floors. Boarded up stalls and dark rooms meet us on our way to the clothes factory, which starts on the fifth floor.

"What if there are more cracks in the walls?" Farah asks. Her eyes flick around, scanning the walls and the staircase and the ceiling, wide and frantic like a mouse's. "If there is, do you think he will send us home? If the offices and shops have closed, why haven't we?"

*He* is our supervisor. A short, pot-bellied man with an angry squint and a high-pitched voice. *There is no crack*, he told us yesterday. *A bit of plaster came off, is all. If you don't go inside and work, not only won't you get your salary in time, you won't get paid at all!*

We know what happens when there is no pay. When mother lost her seamstress job due to a strike, and father was run over by the motorbike, we had no salary for four months. We almost starved. We almost lost the flat. We almost lost my brother Imon, as we couldn't afford his medicine.

No pay means no life.

"Father always said this building wasn't safe," Farah whispers as we trip up the stairs. "They built it like a stack of cards." She glances at me. "Are you wearing the compass?"

My hand wanders to my chest. I feel the metal object under my shawl. "Of course." Father called it his lucky charm. He picked it up from the street one day, thinking a businessman or foreigner must have dropped it. He asked his customers and knocked on doors, but no one recognised it. Mother told him it was broken. The compass hands did not move. Father should take it to a pawnbroker and use the money to get a doctor for Imon.

*It is not broken*, father said. *The hands point south-south-west.* He placed his finger beside three curly, black letters: SSW. *Daksina-daksina-pascima. Farah, Nazia, you know what lies there?*

We shook our heads. Father spoke of foreign concepts in a foreign alphabet in a foreign language. Translating did not help.

*The sea,* he said. *A blue disk, all open. A happy place.* He ran his finger in a half-circle around the bottom half of the compass, from SSW to an E, where the quarter-past mark on a watch would be. *It is a vast place, the sea.* His eyes grew wistful. *Maybe the compass is a sign we should go there.*

We thought something in his mind had broken. We'd heard of the sea, but it was nothing more than a word, an impossible thing, unreachable for the likes of us. Father proved us wrong when he ended that week on a double profit. One would think it was the dry season by the amount of people flocking by his coffee stall. Father saved his extra earnings in envelopes that he hid inside his mattress. *You are looking at the richest coffee-walla in town,* he'd say with a grin. *We can buy our way out of here, to the sea. Get you out of that grey monstrosity.*

One day, six months ago, he forgot the compass under his pillow. He never made it across the street. A motorbike taxi, blinded by the rising sun, saw him too late. Father died before he hit the road.

Farah and I swore we would never leave the compass behind again. We take turns wearing it, tucking it under our shawl so our supervisor can't confiscate it. Today, I am its bearer.

"You think too much." I touch her hand. "Just work, ok?"

Farah pulls her hand back.

Everyone stares at the crack in the wall as we enter the factory room and take our seats behind the sewing machines. It spiders down from a corner halfway to the floor, disappearing behind the stack of cardboard boxes used for packaging clothes. Smaller cracks spread out from it like legs.

Our supervisor wanders down the rows, glaring at anyone who's not in position yet.

I eat a biscuit before I start. I woke up too late for breakfast: mother had already left for work, grandmother was feeding the last morsels of food to Imon, and Farah was waiting for me at the door, telling me to hurry. I popped into the 7-11 shop on the way here and snatched up the closest packet to hand. Pineapple cream sandwich biscuits. My favourite, my father's favourite. I pull the halves apart, licking the cream before taking a bite. The sweet, buttery biscuit crumbles in my mouth, a welcome change to the rice and dried fish we have at home every day. As my supervisor draws near, I stuff the packet into my rucksack and place the fleece I was working on yesterday under the needle. I feel his razor stare on my shoulder as my foot comes down on the pedal and the needle erratically jabs into the fabric. Soon, all that can be heard is the *whirr-whirr* of three hundred sewing machines.

Twenty minutes later, they are silenced. A pulse of light emanates from the lamps and then we are plunged into darkness. Power cut. Confused voices fill the air, met by our supervisor's order to calm down. We do not yet hear the faint rumbling creeping down from above.

Not until the room begins to shake.

Panic builds around me. People rush out of their seats and scramble for the door. Farah is two rows away from me, blocked from view by a pillar. As I call her name someone pushes against me from the side, making me look up.

The building is falling on top of me.


Black. No air, no noise. Only dust, clogging my throat. Breathing sets it on fire. Clamping my mouth shut, I hold my breath, waiting for my body to succumb.

It has other thoughts. One by one my fingers and toes begin to curl, my hands and feet to flex, my arms and legs to bend. They are stiff and sore, but not broken, and as far as I can tell, not bleeding. My right hand wanders up my stomach, registering the even skin and intact ribs, the heart beating as it should be, the throbbing pulse in my throat and the warm breath from my mouth.

*Alive.*

A black, wooden surface, rough and veined against my fingers, sits above me. The sewing table?

I splay my fingers against it and bring all the feeble strength I can muster into my hands. Elbows bend into a push. Two pushes. Three.

With a groan, the table topples over. I sit up.

Pain sears my head.

There's a bald, sore patch of skin amidst the hair. Fingers red when I bring them to my eyes. Looking over my shoulder, I distinguish black tufts of hair trapped between two concrete slabs.

I look in search of the light source. A hole two meters up the debris, letting in a fragile, filigree light, revealing my surroundings.

The bodies crumpled by my legs. One of them missing a head. A third body beside me, hand extended towards my leg, almost touching. A man, his head twisted to the side at a strange angle.

I bite my lip, resisting the urge to pull my legs in, to scramble away and hide. I take the man's hand and hug it. "I'm sorry," I whisper. "I'm sorry you weren't as lucky as me." His fingers are stiff and unresponsive in my palm. Perhaps he was the one who pushed me from the side, when I tried to reach…

Farah.

I crawl over to the left side of the broken room. A wall of debris, wood and cardboard meets my eye, but no sister. No limbs or clothes or hair. The building crumbled like a pack of cards, she could be several meters beneath me.

Three times I call her name, listening to the silence. Then my body folds in upon itself as I sink to the floor, knees to face, rocking back and forth.

The sliding of metal against my skin makes me still. I fish the compass out from under my shawl. It glows faintly in the dark.

*Why me?* I ask it. *Why didn't you save Farah, too?*

A voice drifts through my mind, weightless and distant. *South-south-west, south, south-east….*

My gaze is caught by something beyond the compass. A black object, something red and plasticky flashing inside—

The biscuits.

Within two seconds I've crawled to my rucksack and crammed two biscuits into my mouth. I almost cough them back up. The dust in my throat forbids me to swallow.

I need water.

As if hearing my thoughts, something drips onto my

head. And again, and again, a steady drip. *Rain*. Hitting my face now, drawing wet lines across my skin.

Sticking out my tongue is not enough. As if on purpose, the rain drops land everywhere but there. I need a vessel to guide them.

Letting the compass dangle from my neck, I push myself onto hands and knees. The biscuits may have fired up my brain, but my limbs are still half-conscious. Two crawling steps and I'm already out of breath. The space I'm in is narrower than I first thought. Concrete and rubble scrape against my spine and the sore spot on my head. My hands are eyes, scanning the surface. They close around something slim and cold. A metal pipe. Grasping it, I reach up to the hole, using the slabs as scaffolds to help me stand. I extend my arm and close my lips around the mouth of the pipe.

Never has water tasted more like a blessing. I stay until the skies dry up and the last drop trickles down my pipe. Then I sink back into the filigree grey and eat my third biscuit.

What now?

Faint sounds drift in through the hole. Men, calling and shouting. The muted rumbling of machines.

Twenty-nine stories' worth of concrete and alabaster stand between me and the rescuers. By the time they reach me, I could be beyond saving.

Wouldn't death be mercy?

Movement draws my attention. A shadow, skirting across the face of the compass, showing the outlines of a man I know so well.

*South-south-west, south, south-east.* A wind shimmies down through the hole above me, tickling the bald patch on my head. *East….*

Father would never forgive me if I died here. His daughters buried with his dreams, his lucky charm nothing but a useless trinket.

Death is dishonour. I must hold on, until the men reach me. Clutching the compass to my chest, I repeat my father's mantra, eyes shut, trying to imagine that world of blue. The strip of daylight fades, grows, fades again. I lose track of time. The biscuit packet shrinks in size. Instinct pushes my mind beneath the surface of awareness: I become a creature of the dark, a creature of instinct, scuffling through the tunnels of debris which are now my home, scavenging for scraps of food when my rations are gone. When the rescue men's work sends tremors through the building, I crawl through the concrete tunnels to a safer space, always making sure I have access to the sky. I make a bed for myself out of torn garments and softer mounds of rubble, cradling the compass to my chest, listening to the winds getting louder. Sometimes, the fragment of a male voice whistles with them.

One day, the winds are drowned by a thundering roar. Peeking out through a crack between the slabs I see a monstrous yellow thing with a metal claw, digging up rubble.

Bulldozer. Around it, searching through the debris—

A tremor causes a piece of alabaster to dislodge from the ceiling and hit my shoulder.

I tap the pipe against the concrete. Try to poke my head through the crack so the rescue workers can see me. No sound escapes my lips when I open my mouth. My vocal chords have been unused for so long they've forgotten how to speak. The men drift closer, but their eyes are on the ground, unseeing. Another tremor, another rubble block tumbling.

I tap the pipe and the compass at the same time, creating a broken, discordant rhythm which slows as my wrists tire. I can't keep this up much longer…

Then one of the rescue workers stops dead in his tracks. He stares up in my direction.

"Stop the machines!" The *crunch* of boots against rubble

draws near and then a sweaty face appears in the crack.

Finally, my voice breaks through. "Sir, please help me." The sound is feeble, inhuman.

"Are you hurt?" the man asks.

"No."

A torch is passed through the crack. "Find some clothes. We are going to cut you out."

Only then do I realise I am naked. The rubble must have torn the garments off my body, strand by strand. With the aid of the torch I locate a purple *sari* half buried in the rubble and wrap it around myself.

An ear splintering screech cuts the air. Metal teeth pierce through the concrete, creating new cracks, new splinters of light.

The wall tumbles down. A silhouette appears in the opening, blocking the daylight, grabs hold of me by the elbows and hauls me back into the world of the living. My rescuer cradles me like a baby as he makes his way down the rubble. Noise and movement come at us from all sides; a sea of people, calling, reaching out as if I'm some kind of miracle. As I'm passed through different sets of hands on to a stretcher and carried through the crowd, their chant finally reaches my ears.

God is great.

My eyes close under the blinding sun, my surroundings and my consciousness drifting away on the waves of father's mantra. *South-south-west, south, south-east, east....*

# "Compass of the Winds"

JOSEPHINE GREENLAND is a Swedish English teacher living in Edinburgh, Scotland. Her debut novel *Embers* was started during her MA in Creative Writing at the University of Birmingham, and will be published in early 2021. She plays violin, enjoys running and hiking in the great outdoors, is obsessed with herbal tea, and has a strong affiliation with black cats.

She says: "My story was inspired by the Rana Plaza incident in Bangladesh in 2013 and the real case of a young girl who survived in the ruins for seventeen days. I spent hours reading articles and watching interviews about the event to make my retelling as authentic as possible, and to let the voice of the girl come through strongly in my narrator."

# Appendix 1

# Honorable Mentions

We received hundreds of Huxley submissions to this year's Literary Taxidermy Short Story Competition, and many impressed both early readers and final judges. In the end many good stories were turned away. The following stories all made it to the last round of selection. Keep an eye out for these writers. We're confident you'll see their work in the future.

Jane Andrews, "Tempus Fugitive"
Skip Ashseed, "45 Minutes to Destination"
Tabitha Bast, "There Is Life at This Level"
Susan B. Borgersen, "Strong and Black"
Ned Boyden, "The Department of Sanitation"
Gilbert Ben Brynildsen, "Toothpicks"
Kathryn Crowley, "Lockdown Differences"
Selina De Luca, "Clockwork"
John J. DeDominicis, "Obsession, Lies, and Murder"
Una Dimitrijevic, "American Dreamers"
Carol Josephine Dixon, "Stories"
Brian Douglas, "The Tiger"
Josephine Draper, "Takeover"
Sean Fallon, "The Fido Paradox"
Peter Hankins, "New Troy"
Anna Sara Henderson, "Our Eleemosynary Future"
Paul Hillman-Harris, "Always Sunny"

Caroline Hunt, "The Uncurling"
Suzanne Johnston, "Confidants"
Michael Kuty, "The Other Side of the Lamp"
Claire Lanyon, "The Documenter"
Leah M, "Derelict, Neglect with No Regret"
Bobbie Allen Macniven-Young, "Such People"
Eleanor Musgrove, "The Sixteenth Key"
Jennifer Rathwell, "Taps"
Patrick Roycroft, "Succumbing"
Alexandra Runge, "Building Bricks"
Rachel Marie Salhi, "The Whiskey Heel"
Janeen Samuel, "The Gift of Mrs Burtenshaw"
Michael Seaton, "Drop South"
Rick Shingler, "Dog Run"
Michael Taylor, "Thirty Days Hath September"
Richard Vadim, "One Tin Cup of Freedom"
Rhonda Valentine Dixon, "Amaira's Fortune"

# This Year's Judges

Given our desire for submissions to span genres, we assembled a group of professional writers and editors from all walks of the literary life. The judges for this year's competition included a poet, a playwright, a mystery writer, a speculative fiction writer, a journalist, a hard-SF game designer, a creative non-fiction writer, and a fantasist. They had a challenging task, separating not only wheat from chaff, but wheat from wheat, and we are grateful for their enthusiastic and perspicacious participation.

**Catherine Barnett** is the author of three collections of poems: *Human Hours* (2018), *The Game of Boxes* (2012), and *Into Perfect Spheres Such Holes Are Pierced* (2004). Her honors include a Whiting Award, a Guggenheim Fellowship, and the James Laughlin Award from the Academy of American Poets. She has published widely in journals and magazines, including *The New Yorker*, *The Kenyon Review*, and *The Washington Post*. Barnett teaches in the graduate and undergraduate programs at New York University. She has degrees from Princeton University, where she has taught in the Lewis Center for the Arts, and from the MFA Program for Writers at Warren Wilson College.

**Kelley Eskridge** is a fiction writer, essayist, and screenwriter. She is the author of the New York Times Notable novel *Solitaire*, a finalist for the Nebula, Endeavour, and Spectrum awards. The short stories in her collection *Dangerous Space* include an Astraea prize winner and finalists for the Nebula and Tiptree awards. Eskridge's story "Alien Jane" was adapted for an episode of the SciFi channel series *Welcome to Paradox*. Her film *OtherLife* (2017) is currently streaming on Netflix. She is a former vice president of Wizards of the Coast, the company responsible for the collectible trading games *Magic*™ and *Pokémon*™. She earns her keep as a corporate learning professional, as well as an independent editor with an international client list of established and emerging writers. She lives in Seattle with her wife, novelist Nicola Griffith.

**Dr. Charles E. Gannon** is a Distinguished Professor of English and Fulbright Senior Specialist. His award-winning Caine Riordan/Terran Republic hard-SF novels have all been Nebula finalists and national best-sellers. He is a recipient of five Fulbright Fellowships and Travel Grants and has been a subject matter expert both for national media venues such as NPR and the Discovery Channel, as well as for various intelligence and defense agencies, including the Pentagon, Air Force, Army, Marines, Navy (CNO/SSG and ONR), NATO, DARPA, NRO, DHS, NASA, and several other organizations with which he signed NDAs. (If we told you more about that, we'd have to kill you.)

**Jerry Large** is a recently-retired journalist who—in his weekly column for *The Seattle Times*—wrote for twenty-five years on a variety of topics, including issues of systemic inequality, using history and other social sciences to help understand our society. He joined *The Times* as an editor in 1981 and wrote nearly 1,000 columns during his tenure. Prior to *The Times*, he worked for the *Clovis News-Journal*, the *Farmington, New Mexico Daily Times*, the *El Paso Times*, and the *Oakland Tribune*. Born in Clovis, New Mexico, he holds a B.A. in Journalism and Mass Communications from New Mexico State University, and was a J.S. Knight Fellow at Stanford University. He is currently teaching at the University of Washington Department of Communication.

**Brian Parks** is an American playwright, journalist, and editor. He lives in New York City and served as the Arts & Culture editor at *The Village Voice*, as well as Chairman of the Obie Awards. As a playwright, Brian has produced works that are noted for their dark comedy and fast pace. Best known for his play "Americana Absurdum" (which consists of the two shorter plays, "Vomit & Roses" and "Wolverine Dream"), his other works include "Goner," "Suspicious Package," "Out of the Way," "The Invitation," and "Imperial Fizz." "Americana Absurdum" was honored with the Best Writing award at the 1997 New York International Fringe Festival and a Scotsman Fringe First Award at the 2000 Edinburgh Festival Fringe. He is currently Senior Editor at *4Columns*, a website of arts criticism aimed at a general audience.

**Michael Pronko** is a mystery writer, essayist, and teacher, born in Kansas City, but living and writing in Tokyo for the past twenty years. He has published three award-winning collections of essays: *Beauty and Chaos: Essays on Tokyo*; *Motions and Moments: More Essays on Tokyo*; and *Tokyo's Mystery Deepens*. His award-winning mystery novels *The Last Train*, *The Moving Blade*, and *Tokyo Traffic* feature Detective Hiroshi Shimizu who investigates white collar crime in Tokyo. He writes regularly for many publications, including *The Japan Times*, *Newsweek Japan*, *Jazznin*, *Jazz Colo[u]rs*, and *Artscape Japan*; and runs his own website, *Jazz in Japan*. He is a professor of American Literature at Meiji Gakuin University where he teaches seminars in contemporary novels and film adaptations.

**Nisi Shawl** is an African-American writer, editor, and journalist. She is best known as an author of fantasy and science fiction who writes and teaches about how fantastic fiction might reflect real-world diversity of gender, sexual orientation, race, colonialism, physical ability, age, and other sociocultural factors. Her debut novel, *Everfair*, was a 2016 Nebula Awards finalist, and her short stories have appeared in *Asimov's Science Fiction*, the *Infinite Matrix*, *Strange Horizons*, *Semiotext(e)* and numerous other magazines and anthologies. Her story collection Filter House was one of two winners of the 2008 James Tiptree, Jr. Award. During the ceremony, she was crowned with the Tiptree tiara and given a plaque, a check, a pie, and a ceramic sculpture of a duck.

**Melora Wolff** received her BA from Brown University and her MFA from Columbia University. Her essays and prose poems appear widely in journals and anthologies, including *The Normal School*, *Salmagundi*, *The New York Times*, and *Best American Fantasy*. Her prose has received Special Mentions in Nonfiction from The Pushcart Prizes, several Notable Essay citations in *Best American Essays*, and the Thomas A. Wilhelmus Award in Short Prose. She is the author of *The Parting*, a collection of magical realist flash fictions. She lives and writes in Saratoga Springs, New York and teaches on the faculty of Skidmore College.

# You, Too, May Become a Taxidermist!

All of us at Regulus Press wish to extend our thanks and appreciation to everyone who participated in the 2020 Literary Taxidermy Short Story Competition. Your enthusiasm and commitment far exceeded our expectations—as did the *overwhelming* number of story submissions we received.

If you didn't participate this year and are coming to this collection of stories new to the idea of literary taxidermy, we hope you've enjoyed what you've found. And if you're a writer, we encourage you—the present reader—to become a future literary taxidermist.

This is our third year running the competition, and we're hoping to do it again, so we're looking for writers, both amateur and professional, to stitch together new and imaginative stories. The competition is your chance to get your hands dirty and join the growing community of literary taxidermists.

For the latest on the competition (and to learn more about the possibilities of literary taxidermy), visit:

www.literarytaxidermy.com

We look forward to seeing what you come up with!

"He was a very good-looking young man indeed, shaped to be annoyed. Then he went into the living-room, and sped the dark before the tiny beams that sifted through the little open windows in the panoramas of Paris."
　　　　—DOROTHY PARKER, "DUSK BEFORE FIREWORKS"


"A is for Amy who fell down the stairs. Z is for Zillah who drank too much gin."
　　　　—EDWARD GOREY, *THE GASHLYCRUMB TINIES*


"We went to the Moon to have fun, but the Moon turned out to completely suck. Everything must go."
　　　　—M. T. ANDERSON, *FEED*


"This is the saddest story I have ever heard. She was quite pleased with it."
　　　　FORD MADOX FORD, *THE GOOD SOLDIER*


"All this happened, more or less. One bird said to Billy Pilgrim, '*Poo-tee-weet?*'"
　　　　—KURT VONNEGUT JR, *SLAUGHTERHOUSE-FIVE*

# OPPORTUNITIES FOR
# FUTURE TAXIDERMY

"Young women, let me address you directly. Ishmaels, let's shoot up his beautiful steps like a drug or dream."
—DAVID BOWMAN, *BUNNY MODERN*

"A purple ocean, vast under the sky and devoid of all visible life apart from two minute ships racing across its immensity. I am so happy to be homeward bound, and I am so happy, so very happy, to be alive."
—PATRICK O'BRIAN, *THE WINE-DARK SEA*

"I know your sleep is precious. A warty angler in your pants."
—CHOO 3T FISH, "BLOOD IS BLUE"

"Lesser catching sight of himself in his lonely glass wakes to finish his book. Mercy mercy mercy mercy mercy mercy mercy mercy mercy mercy mercy mercy mercy mercy mercy mercy mercy mercy mercy mercy mercy mercy mercy mercy mercy mercy mercy mercy mercy mercy mercy mercy mercy mercy mercy mercy mercy mercy mercy mercy mercy mercy mercy mercy mercy mercy mercy mercy mercy mercy mercy mercy mercy mercy mercy mercy mercy mercy mercy mercy mercy mercy mercy mercy mercy mercy mercy mercy mercy mercy mercy mercy"
—BERNARD MALAMUD, *THE TENANTS*

"It was as if no one had heard. The salesman thought, once again, that in three hours he would be on land."
—ALAIN ROBBE-GRILLET, *THE VOYEUR*

# OPPORTUNITIES FOR
# FUTURE TAXIDERMY

"One beast and only one howls in the woods by night. See! sweet and sound she sleeps in granny's bed, between the paws of the tender wolf."
—ANGELA CARTER, "THE COMPANY OF WOLVES"

"The ship didn't have a name. I like long stories."
—IAIN M. BANKS, *CONIDER PHLEBAS*

"Amoebae leave no fossils. Swee-eet!"
—TOM ROBBINS, *EVEN COWGIRLS GET THE BLUES*

"She enters, deliberately, gravely, without affectation, circumspect in her motions (as she's been taught), not stamping too loud, nor dragging her legs after her, but advancing sedately, discreetly, glancing briefly at the empty rumpled bed, the cast-off nightclothes. Perhaps today then … at last!"
—ROBERT COOVER, *SPANKING THE MAID*

"My name is Laura Palmer, and as of just three short minutes ago, I officially turned twelve years old! I have to be numb."
—JENNIFER LYNCH, *SECRET DIARY OF LAURA PALMER*

"A is for Amy who fell down the stairs. Z is for Zillah who drank too much gin."
—EDWARD GOREY, *THE GASHLYCRUMB TINIES*

"The child's world changed late one afternoon, though she didn't know it. In a while she would follow."

—NICOLA GRIFFITH, *HILD*

"This I the first time I've worked without a net. Perhaps we wished there was not so much time."

—THOMAS McGUANE, *PANAMA*

"All this happened, more or less. One bird said to Billy Pilgrim, '*Poo-tee-weet?*'"

—KURT VONNEGUT JR, *SLAUGHTERHOUSE-FIVE*

"Until then, he had never dwelled on the pleasures of memory. These things we know, but not what he felt when he went down into his final darkness."

—JORGE LUIS BORGES, "THE MAKER"

"We went to the Moon to have fun, but the Moon turned out to completely suck. Everything must go."

—M. T. ANDERSON, *FEED*

Toni Morrison's

# 124 BELOVED

Selected Stories from the 2020
Literary Taxidermy Short Story Competition

Edited by
MARK MALAMUD

## 34 STORIES / 124 BELOVED

All stories © 2020 by their respective authors
Introduction © 2020 by Mark Malamud
Anthology © 2020 by Regulus Press
Cover art "Tax Vault" © 2020 by Len Peralta *after Mark Eastbrook*

First Regulus Press printing November 2020
Signal Library 10-0202-12-01

Regulus Press, Seattle WA
*www.regulus.press*

ISBN: 0999446294
ISBN-13: 978-0-9994462-9-4
(Regulus Press)

**124 was spiteful.**
↑
**Beloved.**

—Toni Morrison, first and last line from *Beloved*

# CONTENTS

# Introduction

Welcome to *124 Beloved*, the anthology (this side up) that collects the ten prize-winning stories from the Toni Morrison contest of the 2020 Literary Taxidermy Short Story Competition. (If you're looking for the Aldous Huxley contest, you'll need to flip this book over and upside-down.)

Literary taxidermy is a story-writing process that involves taking the first and last sentence from a well-known work (often a novel, sometimes a short story) and then "re-stuffing" what goes in-between those lines to create a new, wholly-original work. The goal of the literary taxidermist is not just to slap someone else's words onto the start and finish of an otherwise stand-alone story, but to take full ownership of the borrowed lines, interpreting (or re-interpreting) them in order to make them seamless, integral, and in fact the *perfect* start and finish for a *new* story.

The origin of literary taxidermy is *The Gymnasium*, a collection of nineteen stories written between 2003 and 2017 that "re-stuff" classic works by Milan Kundera, Thomas Wolfe, Ian Fleming, and others. It was a clear example of creative parsimony on the part of the author (some might call it laziness), leveraging the words of other writers to jump-start the creative process. Yet rather than ending up as a pastiche or spoof of other (granted, far better) writers, the stories turned out to be very much their own thing. And it made one wonder: What would happen if rather than having a single writer tackle the first and last lines of a variety of classic works, you had a *variety* of writers tackle the *same* lines? What would that collection be like?

Which brings us to the anthology you hold in your hands and the competition that produced it. The Literary Taxidermy Short Story Competition, sponsored for the

third year by Regulus Press, invites writers to stitch together their own stories using the opening and closing sentences of specific works of fiction. For the 2018 competition, participants were given three choices: *The Thin Man* written by Dashiell Hammett; *Through the Looking-Glass* by Lewis Carroll; or "A Telephone Call" by Dorothy Parker. For the 2019 competition, co-edited with Paul Van Zwalenburg, they were given *Fahrenheit 451* by Ray Bradbury.

This year, for the 2020 competition, aspiring writers were given two choices: Aldous Huxley's *Brave New World* and Toni Morrison's *Beloved*.

The present anthology (this side up) contains stories from the Morrison contest. That means that every story you're about to read starts and ends *exactly* the same way—with the first and last lines of *Beloved*. Of course *the path* that each author takes from beginning to end is unique—and therein lies a particular thrill of reading these short works: despite sharing a common frame, they are all *different*.

So some of the stories in this collection are dark, some are playful, some are surreal, some rhyme, and some are just *strange*. They cross genres; they cross continents (and occasionally planets); and they vary in style and diction and tone and voice. Reading each one is like getting a peek at the results of someone else's Rorschach test.

The authors are eclectic, too. They range in age from twenty-four to sixty-three. They also span the globe, so you're about to read stories from the United States, the United Kingdom, and Australia. (And that's why you may notice stories written in British and American English—so don't be shocked to find *biscuit* in one story and *cookie* in the next.) The winning author in this year's Morrison contest is Erika Bauer, a teacher in Michigan. But she's no newcomer to literary taxidermy: her first published story, "A Dark and Final Space," was included in last year's anthology, *Pleasure to Burn*. This year's story, "You Know, He Knew, I Said," is even better, bending Morrison's lines to tell a complicated story of love, companionship, and grief.

But there's more to these stories than the pleasure found in their distinction or their differences. Their *similarities* can be just as intriguing.

Yes, you will find a number of tales within this collection focused on resentment—after all, the opening line is *124 was spiteful*.

And the last line—*Beloved*—guarantees there are numerous stories that orbit an object of affection.

But *those* similarities are not particularly interesting. What's interesting are the similarities that appear in story after story that are *unexpected*. For example, this contest received a statistically-improbable number of stories that include apricots, lab experiments, and French kissing. Why? What is it about *those* two lines by Toni Morison that trigger *these* particular narrative neurons to fire?

Literary taxidermy is nothing if not a kind of inkblot test, an invitation to interpret and then riff inside an ambiguous narrative frame. Even if the bizarre similarities that emerge are inexplicable (and really: why *do* so many of the Morrison stories concern apricots?), it shouldn't be a shock that the same input yields similar output. And yet the black box in-between—the human imagination—remains a mystery.

The stories in both anthologies (this one, right-side up, and that one, upside down) were selected by the editors at Regulus Press. The two winning stories were selected by a panel of eight professional-writer judges. After each story, you'll find a short biographical note about the author, and maybe—just maybe—*you* can figure out how they ended up writing the story they did!


Mark Malamud
5 October 2020

# Best Kept Secret

124 WAS SPITEFUL, in a devilish sort of way, with an indelible hint of malice lurking in the corner of his smile. Amanda Drake warmed to the youth immediately and raised her bidding paddle, wondering how, in this day and age, the Rotary Club could continue to call their biggest annual fundraising event a Slave-for-a-Day Auction. But its name was really none of her concern. After all, wasn't she here to secure a strong young man willing to bend the knee, so to speak? It simply was what it was. As swiftly as she had bid, she was outbid. Amanda raised her paddle again, and again. When she finally escorted the young man out of the building at the cost of $800, she considered him a bargain. His name was David.

"I do hope you have your own transportation," Amanda said once out on the street. "It'd be silly of me to call an Uber when you're heading to my house anyway."

"Yeah, I got a car," he said, pointing to a black Dodge Charger halfway down the block. "With the kind of money you just spent on me, I'm surprised you don't."

"I do." Amanda took several steps forward, leaning on her cane. "But I don't drive. Was that your wife who kept trying to outbid me, or simply another admirer?"

"Girlfriend," David answered, donning his sunglasses—inexpensive Wayfarer knock-offs, Amanda noted, but they matched his generic jeans as well.

"I'm sorry I spoiled your plans, David. But today I need you more than she."

"No problem. I could use a break." He paced his gait to match Amanda's labored steps. Upon reaching his car he opened the passenger door.

"It's refreshing to see gallantry is alive and well. Thank you." Clasping her cane, Amanda slid inside.

"I was taught to respect my elders."

"But do you do it out of respect? Or merely because it's expected?"

An Elvis-inspired sneer curled his lip. "Because you recognize the difference, Mrs. Drake, for you it's out of respect."

No matter how the day progressed, she knew he'd suit her purpose and she buckled her seat belt with a smile.

David settled into the driver's seat. "So, what kind of day do I have ahead of me?" he asked while programming Amanda's address into the navigation system.

Amanda stroked the aluminum shaft of her cane and eyed him with just the right amount of daring. "Oh, like your girlfriend, my plans involve a bed." She couldn't see his eyes behind the dark sunglasses, but an apprehensive rise of one brow above the frame accompanied disdain upon his lips.

"I didn't sign up for—"

"Relax, David. You're a little young for my taste. I'm not playing a game of *Fuck, Marry, Murder*. Besides, I've already done all that." She gave him a sly nod. "I just need you to help me clean up the mess."

Again, the well-groomed eyebrow arced and Amanda broke into a full-bodied laugh.

"Such a serious Gus, you are! All I need from you is to finish putting together a planting bed for my kitchen garden. Think you can manage that?"

His relief was audible, and he pulled the Charger into the street. "It's kind of late in the season for a garden, isn't it?"

"At my age, tomorrow is never a promise. You do things

while you can. I don't mind getting my hands dirty now and then. Sometimes I enjoy puttering around the yard a little, and a few days ago, on a whim, I bought what I needed to start a small herb and vegetable garden. I do so enjoy a fresh salad, don't you?"

"Um-hum."

"Andrew—that's my husband—volunteered to build me a raised bed for it, and I thought, How nice! He's actually going to spend the time to make something special for me, like he used to do in our early years. But he cheated. He bought a cheap kit, pre-cut and pre-drilled. All he needed to do was screw it together. But before he did that, he left town and I have dozens of seedlings to plant. So, you see, I need you, David, to help me undo the pickle Andrew left me in."

"Your husband just up and left you?"

Amanda gazed out at the passing scenery. "Not forever. Yet it is what it is, and my seedlings can't wait."

After a long silence, David broke it. "Don't worry, Mrs. Drake. You'll get your garden growing."

Amanda sighed. "Yes. With your help, I will. A garden needs to be tended with love. Without love, it's merely vegetation. Don't you agree?"

"Um, sure."

His lie reassured her, and with a satisfied smile, she relaxed in her seat.

When the navigation system brought him to the wrought iron gates of the fence that surrounded Amanda's estate, David's surprise underscored his question.

"You live here?"

Beyond the gate, at the end of a straight, paved driveway was an apricot-colored Edwardian mansion, completely wrapped on both stories in bright white porches. An expansive lawn lay dappled beneath the shade of old oaks and new maples. Amanda opened the gate with a remote code on her mobile phone. "It's smaller than it looks. A

third of the whole damn house is nothing but porches, but it's home. There's a service road ahead on the left, just past that lilac bush. It'll take us around back so we don't have to walk so far."

After pulling into the parking area behind the main house, David killed the engine and scanned the surrounding yard with his signature disdain. Amanda got out of the car and leaned on her cane. "Over this way, son. It really shouldn't take but an hour. The worst of it has already been done."

A long row of tea roses graced the south edge of a white gazebo off the back of the house. Across a short, sunny expanse of lawn near the back porch, bags of topsoil were mounded beside stacks of lumber. A section of freshly tilled earth, level and free of grass, eight feet long and four feet wide, was blocked off between the posts mounted within each corner.

David scanned the unfinished project. "You could've hired someone to build this for a lot cheaper than what you paid for me, you know. Don't you have a gardener?"

"As luck would have it, his wife died several days ago, so Andrew gave him a few weeks off. Besides, the money went to charity, so…."

David continued to scan the prepped area. "It almost looks like a gravesite."

"Well, that's always a possibility now, isn't it?"

Amanda noted the hostility creeping from his lips again and she laughed. "You don't like me much, do you?"

"I don't believe liking you was a requirement."

"You're right. But I believe we're a lot alike, you and I."

The scorn in his smile was laced with amusement.

Amanda elucidated: "Though you lack money, you portray yourself as wealthier than you are, drawing attention to yourself and seeking respect with your style and choice of car, but you hold people in contempt. I seek respect and

draw attention to myself with an infirmity"—she patted her cane—"and I, too, find most people contemptible. In a roundabout way, we're kindred spirits. That's why I like you." She pointed to the lumber. "The plan called for a bed two planks in height. The wood's all prepared. Once you get those mounted, you can fill it with the topsoil in the bags. There's a drill and some screws on the table. You do know how to run a drill, don't you?"

"I do." David scratched at his chin and stepped over to the table. He glanced back at the freshly tilled soil. "You didn't kill your husband for his money, did you?" He waved his hand toward the house. "For all this?"

Amanda chuckled and hobbled to the water spigot near the edge of the porch. "The house—the money—it was always mine. But his girlfriend didn't understand that."

A slow twist of his neck brought David's hardened gaze back in her direction, and Amanda smiled sweetly in return. She set her cane aside to attach the water hose to the spigot. "Do you really think I killed my husband and buried him here in the backyard for you to cover up?"

David pointed to the bare garden plot. "There's always that possibility, right?"

"It's an interesting idea. Or maybe," Amanda went on, "it's not Andrew that's buried here. Maybe it's his girlfriend. Or maybe, just maybe, it's simply a patch of ground prepped for a kitchen garden." She smiled once more before she shrugged. "Then again, maybe my husband never left town at all and is buried in the garden. Or maybe he left town with his girlfriend and they chose to vanish from the face of the earth. The possibilities are limitless."

David knelt and began to attach the first side plank to the corner posts. "May I ask where your husband is right now?"

Amanda walked, without a limp, to the line of hybrid tea roses at the gazebo, dragging the water hose with her. As she watered the first rose, a creamy Francis Meilland, the

moisture deepened the color of the surrounding mulch, a mixture of the old and the new which she'd sprinkled throughout the rose bed yesterday. "The destination on his ticket was Chicago," she answered. "His flight departed last night, but in all honesty, he could be anywhere by now."

David secured another plank in place.

"However, it is possible," Amanda pinched off a browning leaf from the fragrant Summer Surprise rose, "had I killed him, then he never got on that plane. Yet, if someone were to check, I'd bet they'd find his car at the airport and discover he'd checked in for his flight."

"Did you see him off?"

Amanda moved to the next rose in line, a glowing yellow Winter Sun. "It's quite possible that I purchased his ticket. On his computer. With his credit card. It's quite possible that I drove his car to the long-term parking lot—"

"But you can't drive," David reminded her as he secured another plank.

"Ah." Amanda stepped away from the roses and raised her finger. "I said I don't drive, not that I can't. So, just imagine for a moment, David, that I murdered my cheating husband and buried him in what will become my kitchen garden. Imagine that I then purchased his ticket and packed a small, run-of-the-mill carry-on bag, parked his car in the long-term parking lot, then walked into the airport and checked-in his ticket electronically. Then, perhaps, I went into the ladies room and, because you can't leave your luggage unattended, I took the carry-on with me and once inside a stall, I changed my clothes and then left the airport by a different door, because of cameras, you know. Once back outside, I hopped onto a hotel shuttle. Once at the hotel, I might've walked to a bus stop, then disembarked at a restaurant for an early breakfast before calling for an Uber to take me to the auction—"

"You've really thought this through." David placed another plank.

Amanda moved her water hose to the delicate pink Moonstone rose. "Once or twice in my life. What if instead," Amanda spoke passionately, "Andrew really did fly to Chicago. Perhaps I then sent his girlfriend a message from Andrew's computer and lured her here for a rendezvous. Perhaps, when Andrew returns, he'll never know why she disappeared...or where she went. Yet he'll unknowingly feast upon her with every salad I prepare." Amanda turned and eyed David over her shoulder. His eyes were still hidden behind dark lenses, and he stared back in mute disapproval for a moment before continuing his work. But had it truly been disapproval? Or merely morbid curiosity? She turned back and continued moving the water down the line of roses.

"Don't get me wrong, David. Despite his flaws, I loved my husband, but I will not tolerate betrayal." Amanda glanced toward the sky, taking note of the ominous clouds. "It'll storm before long. With luck it will rain. I find rain refreshing, don't you? It promises new life and washes the bitterness away."

"I'm almost finished." David placed the final plank. "You don't really need that cane, do you?"

"No more than you need your sunglasses. Yet they give you an edge, don't they? An air of mystery, because they hide the truth of your soul. Out in public, my cane also provides me an advantage." Amanda bent to inhale the fragrance of the delectable Peace rose before her. "People show a bit more respect to an older woman with a cane. Without it, I am rather invisible. I don't like being taken for granted."

"You strike me as a woman who knows exactly what she wants and knows how to get it. I don't believe anyone should ever dare take you for granted, Mrs. Drake. Not your husband. Not his girlfriend. Not even your slave for a day."

He set his sunglasses on the table and their eyes met. The intensity lingered with thoughts laid bare. A promise

unspoken. Yet still, she needed to hear it.

"Have you ever cheated on your girlfriend, David?"

"Never," he told her. "I wouldn't much respect myself if I did."

"And if she cheated on you?"

He released a long sigh. "In that case, I guess the possibilities might be limitless." He began to pour the first bag of soil into the garden bed.

"You know," Amanda mused, inspecting her brilliant red Mister Lincoln for aphids, "if one had a foreknowledge of a crime and willingly helped cover up that crime, one could possibly be convicted of…what's that term I want? Not an accomplice. Not a co-conspirator. Oh, I remember now—as an accessory after the fact."

David continued to pour topsoil into the bed in silence. When the last crumbs of dirt fell from the bag, he spoke. "I suppose if he did so willingly, one could." He looked over at her. "That is, of course, if a crime had been committed."

"Yes, David." Amanda turned back to her roses. "If a crime were actually committed."

Amanda moved the water hose to the next rose. A new rose. One of three new roses, planted only yesterday, the trio providing a delightful blend of blood red and cream, blushing white, and vivid, velvety scarlet blooms:

One Dark Night.

One Best Kept Secret.

And lastly, one Beloved.

# "Best Kept Secret"

L.F. FALCONER is a computer operator living in Nevada, in the United States. She is a collector of stones and old glass and an avid gardener, challenging Mother Nature to constant duels. (Sometimes, she says, Mother Nature even lets her win.) She has written seven novels of dark fiction as well as a collection of short stories. Her work has been published in *Weirdbook Magazine*, the *Shallow Waters Flash Fiction Anthology*, and *From the Yonder: A Collection of Horror from Around the World*.

She says: "I never truly know where my stories are going until they take me there, which makes each one an adventure. The first sentence of this year's Literary Taxidermy Short Story Competition was an invitation I couldn't refuse and once the character of Amanda Drake began to take on a life of her own, the entire story fell into place, leaving me with a devious little smile of satisfaction at the end."

Amis Dee

# Submission 129

124 WAS SPITEFUL, and beloved.

•

124 was *spiteful*, down, and *soiled*, across. Lexi bit the end of her pencil. 90 was *decadent*, down, and *deceased*, across. 75 was *rangy* and *rusted*. 62, *putsch* and *puerile*. 58, *cursed* and *cantankerous*. Where had everything gone so wrong? Thirty-five minutes and pretty much everything had gone to hell. She glanced back to the top of the crossword, back to where it had all begun with such promise, where 1 was *beautiful* and *beloved*.

•

124 was spiteful which was a shame. 123 was prideful. 120, the same. "Hullo, 3," said 206. "Move aside," said 67 to a somber 66. Lost key for 111. Package for 44. Here at Cardinal House, numbers adorned both the face and the door. Here at Cardinal House, it had always been the case. It was sadly a colorless decimal place. But one day 7's cat slipped past 7's door, and the cat—on light feet—raced to the end of the floor. 4 happened to open the door at that time, and it was clear this escape was more plan than a crime. And this was the way that 7 met 4, and names were exchanged as never before. This is the way that everything changed, and words replaced numbers, and feelings exchanged. Not just for Pete and Mary, of course, but also their pets—since they were the source—named Love (a tabby) and Beloved (a blue). So for words, neighbors 7 and

4 need only a few. *Pete* and *Mary*, to start, and to follow just two—*Love* and *Beloved*. It's really what counts. And thus Pete and Mary are pleased to announce: from city apartment to heaven above, love and be loved, love and beloved.

•

124 was spiteful, low-cut, and body-hugging—a simple reminder of everything you could never have. A sublime admixture of silk and contempt. Djinna smiled. Such sartorial perfection was rare on the catwalk. "We might sell a few of those," they whispered, and their partner circled the item in her program. "Let's hope, D. Let's hope." 125 was next, a little black number that left little to the imagination. Djinna shook their head. "Too obvious. Over it." "So over," their partner concurred, "so totally *ove*." She struck the item out with a large X. 126 was the color and shape of flame. Djinna's eyes narrowed. As the model moved down the runway, the fiery fabric seemed to lick at her body. "Temptress," Djinna groaned. "Seductress," their partner agreed. "Femme fatale." "Wanton strumpet." "Hot *couture*." "The jezebel look—can't move it." "Won't sell." "So totally *ove*." Their partner returned to the catalog and crossed it out. Djinna looked around. Several people were already standing. Some press, some sponsors, a few celebrities. "Is that it?" they asked. Their partner flipped through the rest of the catalog. No more numbers. Just ads and bios. She sighed, then capped her pen. This was going to be a lean year for *M Alice*, their label. "*Ove*, D."

•

124 was spiteful spiteful spiteful spiteful spiteful spiteful spiteful spiteful spiteful spiteful spiteful spiteful spiteful spiteful spiteful spiteful spiteful spiteful spiteful spiteful spiteful spiteful spiteful spiteful spiteful spiteful spiteful spiteful spiteful spiteful ok beloved.

•

One twenty for Was. Spiteful, he tossed the Franklin back in Father Oswald's face. "I don't need your charity." Oswald shrugged, didn't bother to pick up the discarded bill. He turned to Haskel, next one in line, and peeled off another twenty. This one was received eagerly; and thus Oswald proceeded down the line of workers, one after another, gifting twenty after twenty until he'd given them all away. All, except the one still on the ground at Was' feet. Yes, Was was still there. He could have left, could have stormed off, but he'd stuck around until the end. "I don't need any charity!" he repeated. "Not from you, not from anyone!" Father Oswald sighed. "You will always be welcome here. You will always be loved."

•

124 was spiteful, but you couldn't say he was stupid. Emily had run nearly 300 rats through the maze, but this one—number 124—was the only one to master it. Yet he showed contempt for his human captor, and even the carrot treat offered as a reward at the end of a session was often met with a snarly bite. *Well, two can play that game,* Emily thought, and on Thursday, black Sharpie in hand, she wagged a finger at the rodent, grinned, crossed out his number and gave him a name: *Beloved.*

•

One 24 was spiteful; the other, skillful. You could see it easily the first time you saw either on the football pitch. One kicked at shins to make a point; the other dribbled and outwitted. One complained when the other team scored; the other ran back to the center line and urged his teammates on. Identical numbers on different teams. One was tolerated; the other, beloved.

•

1:24 was spiteful. *And the spies saw a man come forth out of the city, and they said unto him, Shew us, we pray thee, the entrance into the city, and we will shew thee mercy.* But there was no city. The biblical passage was a trick. A trap. But why? Something in our stars? Something in ourselves? Something in our blood? Something in our cells? Simon pleaded before the judge, but the judge was unmoved. Neither one, in the end, was beloved.

•

124 was *Spite*, full of bitter soda that, if you dared to taste, would make your face pucker up and look like that cartoon prostitute on the candy roll right next to it, 147, *StreeTarts*. "A fishy taste for a fishy product," or so its grimy wrapper proclaimed. Next to 147 was 12, *Milky Whey*. "Comes in your mouth, not in your hands." Heh-heh. Some nights Tommy would sit at the foot of his bed and stare at his collection of nearly forty life-sized parody products, collected over years and years (or at least during most of fifth grade). He hadn't opened any of them, of course. That would obliterate their value as collector's items. In fact, he rarely even took them off the shelf. Except for one, which he was drawn towards like no other. The prize of his collection, catalog number 201, smack dab in the center of his display—under the shelf with his baseball mitt and baseball cards, and above the shelf with his collection of Rubber-Man comic books—a mint-condition still-in-the-box squeeze tube of *Johnson & Johnson's Heart Remover*. Its tagline: "Not everyone needs to be loved."

•

124 was spiteful. 125 had terrible spelling. 126 was hackneyed. 127 was incomprehensible. Submission 128 was racist *and* sexist. And 129 was all over the place, yet somehow beloved.

# "Submission 129"

AMIS DEE is a GIS developer living in Arizona, in the United States. She's thirty-two years old, but is proud of her lengthy résumé which includes time as a software editor, a graphics designer, an awkward ballerina, an animator, and a singer in an all-girl karaoke band. She has been published online, but "Submission 129" is her first published short story.

She says: "I didn't know what to do with the Morrison lines. Nothing seemed to stick. I kept starting and giving up. But after a few beers with some friends, I decided why limit myself to just one story? Why not just do them all?"

Khariya Ali

# A Songbird's Silence

124 WAS SPITEFUL. Today even more so than usually.

123 reeks of cheap liquor and stale cigarette smoke, but is a little bored of his task. When he raises his fists, it always seems a bit lacklustre. Poor man can't put his heart into it, and it shows. There are things he'd rather be doing; places he'd rather be. He doesn't have the morality to be repulsed by his task—they drill that out before sending them in—but he has done it for long enough it's nothing of note to him.

125 is newer, you can just tell. In another life he'd have made a fine civil servant. He never pulls punches, but they aren't spiteful. They are clean, efficient, professional. For him it's about a job well done. He could just as diligently wear a suit and file paperwork as break jaws.

124, though, is spiteful. He's the one who will tweak a broken nose, or aim an extra kick at the shins. He'll pull hair and twist it, unable to keep that little bit of a smile off his face as he does. When he comes into the cell, you can tell there's nothing else he'd rather be doing. It isn't a job for him, it's a godsend—an opportunity for a sadist to indulge himself every day and be paid for it to boot.

124 smiled when he broke my ribs, and as the others leave the cell he presses his boot just hard enough to hurt, putting one foot atop my crumpled body like a new land he's claiming for King and Country. I look in his eyes and see a slathering hunger to go further. But he has orders—pain is the name of the game; death isn't. So, he lifts his foot eventually, and walks out, letting the cell door slam shut behind him.

29

The guards don't show inmates their names. They don't even call each other by them in front of us. All an act—ostensibly for security, but who the hell would any of us tell? No, it's about control. They can't make the men who beat us faceless, so they just make them nameless. The King's men are numbers, and we are names. It seems a strange twist of fate that prisoners should have more individuality than their captors—but that is the point, I suppose. It is who we are that landed us here, and it is who we are that they punish. If we had been nameless, kept our heads down, maybe we could be the ones with our boot pressing down into someone else's chest.

So I memorise their numbers. They are stitched onto their uniforms—at the front and on the arm. The 1 on 124's uniform is fraying—the bottom stitches are coming loose. I know that because he likes to get close to my face when he applies the hot irons. Sometimes he whispers in my ear that if I just cry, he'll stop.

When I get out of this place, he'll be the first one I kill—and I'll do it slowly.

There's the sound of a bell ringing faintly in the distance. I hear it chime; once, twice. Lunch time. Interrogation will be over for the morning.

It takes some of the newer prisoners a while to realise it isn't really about information. They go in stubborn as mules, with secrets to protect and noble ideas about courage and justice and honour. They will be martyrs, they think, for the great and noble cause. They will be the stuff of legends and songs and history books.

If the only purpose of all of this was to take our lives, maybe they would be right. But we don't die here—not until we've slipped out of memory, and out of the potential of redemption. Not until we've yielded our secrets and begged for death over and over and over. Not until we've betrayed our friends, and our beliefs, and we no longer believe in any salvation.

The medics will be here soon, ready to pull inmates from cells and patch them back together, just well enough to be pretty sure they won't die. Then back to the interrogation tomorrow.

They've stopped even asking me questions. I'm glad—we've dropped pretence. They want to see us defeated, humiliated, broken. Every blow, every burn, every cut: "this is what happens when you step out of place." Our crime isn't really trying to kill the King—it's daring to want to. There are grand men who have ordered the world just so, we presumed to challenge their authority, their decisions, so they take our choices, and leave us only their control.

The door opens with a groan.

"Morrison!" It's 124 again, now accompanied by the medic—a twitchy little man I've not seen before. "Why don't you tell Doc where it hurts so he can make it all better?"

Bastard. No doubt my gaze burns with hatred as I struggle up into a sitting position, collapsing against a wall and panting from exertion. I flash him a smile though, showing bloody teeth.

The medic stumbles back a little, alarmed by my expression. 124 laughs and claps him on the shoulder. "Don't worry, Doc, just our little joke there. This songbird, she ain't been singing in a long time." He chuckles to himself at his own supposed cleverness. Moron.

The medic stares at him blankly.

"God, man!" 124 exclaims. "You must be green—you never heard of Wren Morrison?"

The medic's eyes finally light with understanding. A vainer me from a past life might have been offended that he didn't recognize me. But I can't very well hold that against him—I don't exactly look my best. He's seen the videos, and the posters—of course he has. I watch him take in my emaciated form, and disfigured face. I can see the mental calculation as he tries to work out where the Songbird of the

Revolution is hiding in this wasted, walking corpse. Then he remembers what they did to me—he probably saw that, too. After all, it was televised.

"Don't worry, Doc." 124 continues, smiling at me maliciously. "She's no danger to anyone anymore." He pushes past the medic and sits himself down on the bed in my cell, crossing his legs and leaning back.

One day I will prove him wrong.

The medic shuffles over timidly, but stops short of me and looks nervously to 124, a question clearly on his mind.

"Hurry it up, Doc," 124 groans. "We've got more to see after this." He strides over to where I sit and pulls me up by my hair. My hands go up instinctively and I claw at his knuckles impotently to try to ease the grip that drags me up. My ribs protest, vociferously. "Just broken ribs and a few burns," he tells the medic. "Set them, bandage them, and we can go." He tosses me like a ragdoll onto the bed where an animal groan escapes my lips.

The medic pales, but he sets about his work. His hands flutter with apprehension as he puts them to my injuries, but I can't fault his handiwork. His eyes avoid my face—I prefer that over the grim fascination some of his predecessors have watched me with. It hurts when he sets my ribs—three were broken—but he does it fast and deftly.

My mind wanders as he works—it often does. There is nothing in my world anymore to keep my mind from wandering—and I would not wish to stop it, the paths it walks are much more pleasant than those of reality. I don't know how long I've spent here. I have no way of counting the days. Others in solitary confinement, it is said, talk to themselves. I have heard of people who produced their *magnum opus* inside prison walls, but I am forbidden pen or paper. I can only think to myself.

Perhaps it will make me mad—at the very least my mind teeters on the knife edge of sanity. I cannot speak, and I cannot even write, so there is nowhere for all the words

inside of me to go. They beat furiously at the walls of my brain, desperate to be heard—caged birds with frantic wings.

The King took my voice with his own hands, and now his prison guards work to make my mind follow suit. My thoughts are always clamouring over one another—they trip and stumble and crowd for space and attention— sometimes I think my head will split. I am stitched together by the medics, but the only thread holding the shredded fragments of my sanity together is *vengeance*.

Is that ignoble?

Once, my values would have told me to say *hope*. I believed in hope. I sung about hope before, and those songs inspired men and women to fight. But they killed hope a long time ago. They left ashes where we hoped to plant new seeds. Now I hold on for the chance to make ashes of men like 124.

"Is that too tight?" the medic asks as he fastens the last bandage, directing the question to 124. People do that often—like when they cut out my tongue, I turned deaf.

124 shrugs. "Who cares? Not like she's about to complain—are you Morrison?"

I bristle, but I say nothing.

The medic gathers his bag and walks to the door. 124 remembers my food as he walks out—it is on the cart with everyone else's. He grins at me as he places the bowl of gruel on the floor where he knows I will have to bend to get it.

Like I said, spiteful.

The door closes, but I know he will be watching me on the live camera feed as I struggle across the cell to pick up the paltry meal. My eyes flicker up to its unblinking red light, nestled into the smooth surface of the wall, ever watchful.

There are no windows to my cell. There is only the door. All the walls are smooth concrete—no purchase for fingers to find. The bed is concrete too, with a single sheet for warmth. Toilet breaks are twice a day—the guards enter to

watch when the foul-smelling latrine emerges briefly from the wall. Occasionally I am allowed to wash, carried blindfolded to a communal shower that runs either scorching hot or freezing cold, and doused with soap to prevent lice.

When they come for interrogations, they bring chairs—so they can make us sit. But they take them with them when they leave.

The bowl my food is served in is plastic, there is no cutlery.

The lights run the length of the ceiling, and are flush with concrete so there is nothing to grab—too high anyway to be reached. Sometimes they leave them on at night—I suspect that's also 124.

I slide down the edge of the bed onto the floor, pausing for a breath before shuffling across to the bowl. The movement hurts, but I am too hungry not to make the journey. I sit and sip at the bowl of tasteless watery sludge. Of course, being without a tongue means most things are tasteless. They feed me here to keep me alive, but not enough to keep me strong. And it tasted like shit even when I did have a tongue.

The bowl cleared, I struggle back to the bed, where I lie down and stare at the concrete. Its smooth, unbroken surface should offer a blank canvas to the imagination. I would like to look at it and dream of blue skies and starry nights, but instead its smoothness discomforts me, and my eyes rove it constantly for non-existent fault lines, flaws and fissures.

I know this cell—how many paces from wall to wall, how many handspans across the bed, how many finger-widths the door is made up of. This is my world—tiny as it is, and my body is trapped here as my words are trapped in my head. My words, though, still put the futile fight against their prison walls; my body has long since realized the pointlessness of that.

When they first brought me here, I shouted and screamed and beat the walls. I tried to strangle guards with my sheet, I raked them with my nails and bit and spat. I sang, and I heard the inmates across the prison clamour in response.

Then the King cut out my song, and silence is all that reigns here now.

God, my ribs hurt. The bandages are too tight. They press too hard and the pressure makes it hard to breathe— especially as I lie down. My fingers move to the knot the medic tied, to try to loosen it. My hands are clumsier than they once were. The knot was tied too well and it takes me time to coax it free. I hate that I fumble now, lacking the dexterity that once came so easily.

The cloth slips free and I let it loosen and give a little, my breathing easing as the pressure subsides, but as I adjust the wrappings, my finger catches on something that doesn't feel right. My thumb brushes it again and I freeze. It feels like paper. Is it a hallucination? Have I finally lost the last vestiges of my sanity?

I pull my sheet up a little, and shift, angling my body towards the wall and away from the camera.

It *is* paper, a small piece lodged in the folds of the bandage that I work loose very gently. Curiosity near overwhelms me. Was it an accident? Why is it there? The questions come in a flurry, fast and fluttering. Gingerly, half-unsure, I unfold the paper and—holding it in my cupped hand out of sight of the ever-watchful eye—I read it.

My heart races, my hands tremble. But I smile.

There are four words written on the scrap of paper.

*We are coming, Beloved.*

# "A Songbird's Silence"

KHARIYA ALI is a paralegal living in London, in the UK. "A Songbird's Silence" is her first published short story.

She says: "The title was the last part of this story to be written. The rest was the occupation of a bright afternoon in May, and the copious free time afforded by lockdown. I've always been fascinated by the written word as an immersive experience; its ability to carry you away and draw you in, leaving you wanting more by the time it releases you. I was able to enjoy a small piece of that while Wren and her world coalesced on paper, and I can only hope that there is equal enjoyment for you in reading it."

Michael R Goodwin

# The Wiseman Bridge

124 WAS SPITEFUL.

His real name was Daniel Blau, but he insisted that everyone call him 124. He had the number tattooed on his arm, and said he got it at Auschwitz. None of us questioned him on what he wanted to be called or even where he got the tattoo. There were five of us who lived under the Wiseman Bridge; we all had reasons why we were there, and we all used nicknames instead of the ones we were born with. None of us were in the position to be judgmental.

After 124 had been with us for a few days, I remember thinking that something must have gone terribly wrong in his life for someone like him to wind up under the bridge with the rest of us. He was a smooth talker, charismatic with a kind of confidence that made everything he did seem effortless. He seemed like the kind of guy who would have had it all. His disarming persona earned him a spot with us under the bridge, even though most weren't fond of newcomers.

As I said, he was spiteful, but only when he was being protective of his things. Most of us were a bit possessive as well, being those who had very little by way of earthly possessions at this juncture of our lives. The difference with 124 was that he'd become violent when anyone touched his things. To avoid his mean streak, we all learned to give him a wide berth.

Well, most of us did.

124 always had a cigarette between his lips, but he never

smoked it. Sometimes, late at night, he'd take a beaten-up brass Zippo out of his pocket, flick it open, and stare into the flame. He would hold it just out of reach of the cigarette. Two weeks passed, and he performed this ritual every night. Not once did I see him light his cigarette.

Curiosity got the better of me one night, so I asked him.

"How come you never light it?"

124 jumped, my question startling him. He spun around and in the moonlight I saw something change in his eyes. His pupils were hugely dilated, but they quickly shrunk down to normal size. He smiled.

"Trying to quit, I suppose," he said.

"I've never seen you smoke," I replied.

"That's the thing, Clifford. It doesn't matter what your vice is. Once an addict, always an addict."

He had a point. A lot of us were down here because of a vice. For me, it was alcohol, and like a lot of other alcoholics I knew, I professed that it wasn't my fault that I wound up under the Wiseman Bridge. The things I saw at war came first, and the alcohol came second. Putting the bottle before the family I came home to was third. Whatever path led to the Wiseman Bridge, it was a destination that equalized us all.

"Seems to me like it'd be easier to quit smoking if you didn't always have a cigarette in your mouth and a lighter in your pocket," I countered.

"Some habits are harder to break," 124 said with a shrug. He held up his Zippo and waggled it in the air. "Besides that, Beloved here has seen me through a lot. I just can't seem to part with her."

"Beloved?" I asked.

He nodded. "Mm-hmm. That's what I call her."

The lighter looked similar to one that I was issued in the Army, back before I saw the things that changed me. 124 placed it between his index finger and thumb and spun it

around, the moonlight glinting off the sides.

"Not sure what makes it so special," I said. "Looks like one I used to have."

124 laughed. "Yours was not like this, I guarantee it."

"What makes it so special, then?"

While he considered my question, 124 stuck his cigarette behind his ear and stood up. I thought at first that he was going to walk away, but instead he flipped the lighter open. He thumbed the flint and the wick sprang into flame. He carried it over to me, cupping his hand around the flame so the wind wouldn't snuff it out.

"Look at it," he said reverently.

I looked at his face, wondering if he was serious. It was hard to tell, darkness now obscuring his face, but I decided to indulge him.

"What am I looking for?"

"Just hush, you'll see," 124 said.

He brought the lighter closer to me and I stared at it, watching the flame dance from side to side on the wick. Some time passed, and I was about to tell 124 that I was done with his little game when I saw her.

A woman stepped out from behind the flame like it was a curtain. She was more beautiful than any woman I had ever seen in my life. She was made of fire, her hair flowing upward as it glowed red, orange, and yellow. Her eyes were white hot coals, hips swaying seductively as she consumed the air around us. The woman, this stunning Phoenix, grew larger.

I was afraid at first, which soon mixed with an overwhelming feeling of completeness. I was wholly sustained, having no need for anything. The hunger in my stomach was gone. The itch in my brain that only a stiff whiskey could soothe fell quiet. I felt like a dry riverbed receiving water after a drought.

The woman in flames, now standing nearly a foot tall,

extended her hand towards me. Her lips moved, but instead of hearing words I saw images in my mind. I was simultaneously terrified and entranced by her and by what I saw in my mind, and was frozen in place. I felt the heat radiating from her as she leaned down to touch my face.

124 snapped the Zippo closed, and the Phoenix disappeared.

I began to protest, but 124 placed his hand on my shoulder. His grip was strong and caught me off balance. I fell onto my back and he pinned me down, his knee digging painfully into my gut.

"What did you see?" he demanded.

I closed my eyes, replaying what the Phoenix had shown me. I tried to speak, but I found there was no air in my lungs. They felt dry and burnt. I gasped, and the cool night air filled me.

"I saw the sky on fire," I said at last.

He released his grip on my shoulder and stood up, seeming relieved.

"Did you recognize anything? Anyone?"

I shook my head.

Silence fell between us, and for a few minutes the only sounds were of the Androscoggin River babbling and the idle chatter coming from around a barrel fire nearby. The other Wisemen were huddled around it for warmth in a painful display of our stereotype.

"Who is she?" I asked.

"She's my Beloved," 124 answered simply. "She gives me everything I need."

I nodded because I understood. She made me feel the same way when I looked into her flames, but there was something 124 wasn't saying.

"What does she ask for in return?"

124 didn't offer an explanation, as he knew I didn't need one. I already knew what she wanted, because I had seen it

in my head when she spoke to me.

He got up and returned to his spot under the bridge. I returned to mine, all at once exhausted and my mind filled with roiling flames. I unrolled my sleeping bag and crawled in, falling asleep almost immediately.

I woke up to the sounds of shouting and a scuffle.

The sun was rising and the clouds were low, making the sky look like it was on fire. I shivered as a wave of *déjà vu* passed through me. The sky looked exactly as it had in my head the night before, when the Phoenix spoke to me.

"Give it back!" 124 yelled.

He was on the ground, wrestling with the Wiseman that we called Lincoln, so named for his tall stature and penchant for honesty. Lincoln had something clutched in his fist, and was trying to prevent 124 from prying it out.

"It's mine, I found it!" Lincoln cried.

"No, you stole it!"

Lincoln was even less likely to steal than he was to lie (and he never lied), so it was odd to me how he came to possess whatever 124 claimed was his. They fought with each other while the rest of the Wisemen, myself included, gathered round. We didn't intervene; no one ever did when fights broke out. I leaned in close, trying to see what Lincoln had in his hand. Just then, 124 got one of his fingers hooked inside Lincoln's fist and yanked. His fist sprung open and a small metal object went flying: 124's brass Zippo. I shot out my hand and caught it.

124 watched it fly into my hand and scrambled away from Lincoln towards me. He came up and demanded his lighter back as Lincoln, rubbing at a trickle of blood coming from his nose, retreated to his camp.

The Zippo felt comfortable in my hand, like it had belonged to me my entire life. The way I felt when the Phoenix looked at me, that feeling of wholeness, slowly crept back in. I opened my mouth to refuse giving it back, but 124 spoke before I could get the words out.

"She's *mine*," he said coldly.

At that point in my life, I had lived under the Wiseman Bridge for longer than I had been away at war. During my time at war, I learned how to read a man's eyes. It was a survival technique, a tool in my belt that my time under the Wiseman Bridge honed until it was razor sharp. There's a certain look that a man gets in his eyes when he realizes that he's got nothing left to lose...or nothing left to live for. If it hadn't been for what I saw in 124's eyes in that moment, I wouldn't have given the lighter back.

"I know she's yours," I said, scared of what 124 would do if I refused. "I wasn't going to keep her."

I held the lighter out in my palm, and 124 snatched it away. He shoved it deep into the front pocket of his tattered pants and stalked off.

He disappeared for the rest of the day, coming back just as dusk was settling in. I couldn't help but observe him from a distance, trying to ignore the jealousy I felt at seeing the lighter in his hands instead of mine.

As I had seen him do many times, 124 plucked the cigarette from its perch behind his ear and put it in his mouth. He flicked open the lighter and held the flame out to the cigarette. I expected him to hold it out and stare into the flame like he normally did. Instead, he brought the flame under the cigarette and inhaled deeply.

"Finally give in?" I asked. "Decided you needed a smoke?"

He turned to look at me. His eyes were dead, distant.

"No, she did."

"Who did?"

"Beloved."

His behavior was unsettling, so I turned to walk away. 124 grabbed my wrist and pulled me back.

"Beloved gets hungry every now and then," he said, his speech stilted and disjointed. "That's the thing about her,

and with all fire, really. Once you start to feed her, once she gets reminded of how good it feels to burn—well, she's fire. She's always going to want more. She's going to burn everything until there's nothing left."

His words chilled me. I knew them to be true because of the other things I saw in my mind when the Phoenix had spoken to me. That spiteful streak, that wild spitefulness we all feared was coming. I tried to backpedal away, yanking my arm down to slip out of his grasp.

124 walked away, a trail of cigarette smoke encircling his head like a crown. I took a few steps back, my heart pounding in my ears.

He pulled out a glass bottle from his pocket as he approached Lincoln's camp. He opened it and poured half onto Lincoln, who was asleep under a blanket. He then took a swig, spilling most of what was left down the front of his jacket in the process.

The distance between 124 and I seemed to grow as I ran towards him. I shouted at him to stop, but when I saw the Phoenix appear in 124's hands I knew it was too late. 124 flicked the cigarette onto Lincoln's blanket, the tip glowing cherry red, and the blanket erupted in flames.

The sound of Lincoln screaming echoed up the Androscoggin. He tried rolling to extinguish the flames, but only succeeded in tangling himself up. The fire around him grew as other objects caught on. The acrid smell of burning flesh filled the air. Lincoln stopped screaming as fire blessedly overcame him.

124 turned to me, the Phoenix dancing in his hands.

"He shouldn't have taken my Beloved," he said.

124 looked like he was going to say something else, but the Phoenix, his Beloved, reached out with her fiery hands and grabbed onto his jacket. Flames licked eagerly at the alcohol that he had spilled on himself and fire spread over him instantly with a percussive rush.

The heat kept me back, but there was nothing that could

be done anyways. I held my jacket over my face as black smoke poured up into the night sky.

124 made no sound as he burned. After a few minutes he dropped to his knees, and then fell over on top of Lincoln. The Phoenix consumed them both.

Doc and Simon, the other Wisemen, rushed in with blankets to smother the flames to no avail. When the inferno eventually died down, Doc rolled Lincoln and 124 over to see if by any chance either of them were still alive. They weren't.

The Zippo fell out of 124's hands when they rolled him over. It bounced off the gravel and landed at my feet. I picked it up, expecting it to be hot to the touch. Instead it was quite cool.

I turned and walked back towards my camp. I opened the Zippo and flicked the flint wheel. The Phoenix stepped out of the flame and spoke to me.

She was mine now, she said.

Mine.

Beloved.

# "The Wiseman Bridge"

MICHAEL R GOODWIN is a tax and regulatory specialist living in Maine, in the United States. In addition to writing fiction, he enjoys photography and composing music. He prefers to write in the dark while listening to classical music (usually Mozart's Requiem in D Minor). "The Wiseman Bridge" is his first published short story.

He says: "Inspiration for this story came from the definition of the word spiteful: 'showing or caused by malice.' It made me consider what would drive someone to allow themselves to be overcome, even temporarily, by a desire for evil. With that in mind, I wrote this story in one go, sitting at my kitchen table with a glass of whiskey."

Julia Jordan

# The Salvation of 1-2-4

1-2-4 was spiteful
She snarled and swiped and hissed
She scratched me as I picked her up
This cat will not be missed

Other cats who had been lost
Were waiting to be found
It was a normal afternoon
Of life here at the pound

We walked past all the cages
Of cats still in their prime
Unfortunately for 1-2-4
She'd now run out of time

We took a right past 1-0-1
A sweet and mellow cat
I looked at 1-2-4 and said
"You should have been like that!"

I took her down a hallway
To her impending doom
Left then right then left again
To the injecting room

But then the sound of little feet
And giggling did I hear
As 1-2-4 re-scratches me
A boy and girl appear

"Can we see that cat?" they said
"We'd love one just like her"
And to my shock I heard a sound:
1-2-4 began to purr!

That cat jumps from my arms to theirs
They pat her in delight
I hope she will not scratch them
No; she plays with all her might!

The kids and cat were boisterous
I was pushed around in jest
I pondered as I stumbled back
"These kids bring out her best!"

I thought again and smiled now
As I was once more shoved
1-2-4's not spiteful
She just needed to be loved

# "The Salvation of 1-2-4"

JULIA JORDAN is a part-time non-profit grant writer living in Melbourne, Australia. Although trained as a lawyer, she now spends most of her time raising two small children. Her favorite things include sunshine, porch swings, baked goods, and her family. "The Salvation of 1-2-4" is her first published work.

She says: "I have a two-year-old and a four-year-old, and my days are filled with picture books and toddler songs—so it is not surprising that my literary taxidermy features animals and rhyming verse! The idea came to me on a sleepless night, and the poem was tweaked over many subsequent nights as my mind travelled through the alphabet trying to find the right words to rhyme together."

# You Know, He Knew, I Said

124 WAS SPITEFUL. Tracing the route of modern I-40, NM 124 kicked dirt and nostalgia into the face of the interstate. It was open and worn and reckless, like an artifact, daring us to touch it, to feel the heartbeat of Route 66 thunder up through the tires, pulsate through the steering wheel and into the cabin—oxygen that was dirty and pure. Driving through McCartys, New Mexico, the wheel of the Chevy Chevelle loosely gripped in his left hand, James looks out at the horizon, once again seemingly bewitched by the Zuni Mountains, just west of our destination in Grants, fixated by the lava flow, the *malpais*, all around us. Out of the corner of my eye I watch him roll down his window and put his hand flat against the wind. I know the sensation: all that nothing that feels like something right in the palm of your hand.

Leaning against the passenger window, I watch as 124 curves to the south. I try to read James' eyes but it's hard. The late afternoon sun is ruthless and his profile is unrelenting. We haven't spoken much since Tucumcari, both of us sober and entranced by waves of heat melting the road ahead, an urban mirage made more magical by a terrain so vastly open. And though we haven't spoken and it's quiet, except for the hum of the Chevelle, it's not a quiet that waits for words to fill it. Me and James, we finish each other's silences.

That's how I know that James needs a drink—because I need a drink—a little something to smooth the rough places beneath the surface of his jaw. We have a gig later that night

53

in Flagstaff, but that's still hours off.

First, there's Grants.

I reach over and put my hand on the back of James' neck. Today is an anniversary, the only one he celebrates, and I know that the closer we get to Grants, the more his hands will betray him, the more the muscles in his jaw will twitch, some mystery of biology that only men learn how to do. So even though I've heard the story before, I ask him to tell it to me again.

"Tell me how you met, that night out in the desert. Pretty, the way you always do," I ask. I roll down my window and light a cigarette, inhale slowly while he thinks about it. I pass it to him, lipstick-stained and ready, the way we both like it.

James takes a long drag and the road becomes a slight hill and the sun falls imperceptibly lower in the sky. He looks at me with a silent question, looking for the place to start. I run my hand through his hair, slowly, waiting, until he finds the way.

"I was coming home after playing a late set in Albuquerque," he says. "One of those dark bars named after a woman, full of men. You know the type, Layla. Our kind of place." He laughs and I lean my head back against the seat, picturing the bar and James and the darkness. "You weren't there that night. You were back at that shitty motel, sick. So I played that night alone. It was strange from the beginning, you know?"

"Yeah, I remember," I say, not because he's really asking, but because this is his story, and his story has a rhythm. I look toward the mountains, expansiveness and isolation all around us, James' voice like a map to an unmarked road.

"After the set, I'm packing up my gear and these guys offer to buy me a round. They introduce themselves. Tough guys, Layla. You know, like South Side Chicago meets John Wayne, if you can believe it. But I'm thirsty and it's late, so

I let 'em." I picture James that night—dark jeans, black boots, short thick hair standing up in rebellion. Stubble on his face. That scar about his left eye that you never forget.

"So we're drinking, me and these guys, and I notice him for the first time—Mick. He's sitting around the L of the bar—shorter build, all shoulders and chin, something in his eyes that tells you there's probably a box of shells in his glove compartment. And he's looking at me. Looking at me in that way when you know someone's doing everything not to look at you. And he's got this blond on his arm, and she's holding on to him just so as not to fall shitfaced on the floor. And Layla," James pauses here, like he always does, because he doesn't have the words. No matter how many times he tells it, he doesn't have the words. "When he looked at me, I couldn't fucking breathe. I'm holding this whiskey and laughing at some shit the guy next to me is saying, and he looks at me, and all of a sudden I can't breathe."

And I can see it, James and Mick—James like some cowboy who stumbled into a Calvin Klein ad, those lanky muscled arms, that quiet indifference; Mick like a young Jack Dempsey, a face made more handsome by bruises and scars, that reckless punch.

"So it's getting late, and the guys are leaving, and I got nowhere to be, so I order another shot. The guys pat me on the back, tell me to come around next time I'm in town, make a couple jokes about all the shit they're gonna take when they get home to their girls. And Mick and the girl he's with, she's putting on her sweater, and he walks up to me to shake my hand, and he says, 'Take it easy, man.' And I grab his hand, Layla, and my heart is pounding so loud I swear you can hear the bass. And you know I'm not shy, so when I shake his hand, I really touch his hand and I say, 'You too,' and the sleeve of my jacket brushes his chest when I turn. Like I could feel it."

James stops for a second because he's said a lot, said it in a way he wouldn't normally say out loud. But then he sees me. It's just me. And he goes on, the sun over 124 just

beginning to haze as we head past Anzac.

"He walks out the door, arm around the blond, and I watch him go, like that—me, just nursing that last double whiskey. After a while it gets quiet, and you know how I hate last call, so I head out. I walk to the Chevelle, inhaling that desert air and the cigarette in my hand. I stop in front of my door, just looking at my reflection in the glass, smoking, when I see this shadow over my shoulder. And as I'm getting ready to turn around, his puts his hand on my shoulder, like he owns it, and he says, 'So…where we going?' I turn around and I don't say anything and it's so fucking loud in my head and he says, 'I had to get rid of them. You know…the guys, the girl. Took a few minutes.' And there's this long moment where I'm looking at him, just looking, and then I reach for the back of his neck and he hesitates, flinches for a second, looks around him like a criminal, and when he looks back, I see it. It's like his eyes jump forward. And he grabs me the second before I grab him, and I kissed him in the parking lot, kissed him like we were fighting, cigarette still in hand, kissed him the way you claw yourself back to sleep when you're getting to the good part. When you don't want to wake up."

James reaches for the cigarette again and I can't tell if the story's over because I know all the endings. I know how James drove Mick back to our motel that night, how I could hear them through the paper walls of the motel room— laughing and loud, quiet and pretend-motionless. I know how James dropped him back off at his car the next morning, the way the sun glinted off the windshield as they said goodbye, how every time James played at the bars, there'd be this song that I know he played for Mick, wherever he was. I know how they saw each other that year whenever we drove through New Mexico, how James, who was always bold, always what he was, wanted to hold him in broad daylight. And how Mick, no matter how beautiful James was, would only say it when they were alone.

The blankness of Route 66 gives way as we enter Grants.

We pass the Junkyard Brewery and head into Downtown—
a right on 1st avenue, another right on Roosevelt. Five
minutes tops and we'd be there. I wait a bit before asking
the question because it doesn't feel right to talk about Mick
while there's a fucking AutoZone or Pizza Hut in the
backdrop. But we're almost there and so I ask him right
before we turn onto 1st, while the mountains are still to our
left, while there's still something beautiful to look at.

"Are you ready to see him?"

James looks in the rearview mirror, runs his hand
through his hair. "Yeah," he says. "I'm ready." And then,
"You can come too."

"Always," I say.

We turn onto Roosevelt and ease into the parking lot.
James gets out of the car. By now it's closing in on the final
breaths of sun, daylight burning like whiskey—slow and
steady. I follow James to the meeting spot, always close
behind until we see Mick. I find a big oak tree a couple
dozen paces behind James and sit down, pull another
cigarette from my jeans.

James walks up to the spot and I look out at the trees, so
green after so many mountains. "Sorry I'm late," he says,
and sits down on the grass. He puts his hand against the
gravestone, and then his forehead, and I don't need to look
to know that he's whispering. I don't need to listen to know
what he says. He doesn't cry because it isn't him, but he
holds his chest tight and the muscles of his forearms are
stiff. Someone passing by might think he's trying to rip a
chunk of concrete from the top of the slab, his fingers more
than just holding on in the dipping sunlight.

From beneath the tree, I can see portions of the
headstone, "Michael," "1977," "Beloved son and brother."
I watch as James traces the name with his finger. When he
comes to the word "Beloved," he hesitates, his whole body
caught in the inhale. I know James, so I know he's thinking
about the funeral, his place in the back, how no one there

knew who he was, how he couldn't tell them because Mick didn't tell them.

Time, no matter what anyone says, is irrelevant. How long or how short. Love takes nothing. But I don't say this to James. He lets me sit here because I don't say obvious shit to him, or tell him it's going to be ok, or promise him that this too will pass. I watch him touch the word again and stand up in front of Mick's grave.

"Such a bullshit word, you know?" he says. "A word you hear at fucking weddings and gravesites. No one says it in real life. It feels strange to say it in real life. *Beloved*." He says it like a curse.

I walk up behind him, lean against his back, pull the collar of his shirt down, and kiss the back of his neck lightly. I keep leaning against him, letting the word wash over me, too. Whispered. Archaic. Made only for stone. And before I nudge his elbow, telling him it's time to go, I lean in closer.

"You know, he knew," I say. "Even if you never said it."

And James, like 124, like always, walks away—with me.

"Come on, Layla."

We head back to the Chevelle—James in front, me a step behind. I watch James' silhouette move against the New Mexican horizon as the sun sets, wondering where we'll sleep tonight, wondering if we'll sleep tonight.

Back on Route 66, Grants a few miles behind us, I look toward the darkening skies of Black Rock ahead. James rolls down his window and inhales the night like it's more than oxygen. I pass him a cigarette so he can breathe. Dusk rolls in like there's no need for another sunrise.

I wonder how the darkness can be this soft.

James thinks of Mick. I think of James. The fading, open road thinks of nothing. And everything aches to say what cannot be said: looking ahead, lost behind, words be damned.

Beloved.

# "You Know, He Knew, I Said"

ERIKA BAUER is a teacher in Michigan, in the United States. Stephen King was the soundtrack of her childhood, and her first short story as a teenager was inspired by Anne Rice. Her first published story, "A Dark and Final Space," was a finalist in last year's Literary Taxidermy anthology, *Pleasure to Burn*, and this year's story is even better: we loved its sad yet romantic arc, the tender voice of her narrator, and the deft way she interpreted Morrison's first and last lines. The story was a thrill to read and a pleasure to award.

She says: "Though I've never driven down Route 66, I know it like the back of my hand—the dust, the wind, the expanse—all of it more than nostalgia. Closer to home than home. I was Layla in another life because I'm not creative enough to make this up. I was taught to 'write what you know.' Well, I know this place. I've always known this place."

David Kerekes

# The Missing Husband

124 WAS SPITEFUL. After all these years it has remained so. But I'm straight in my head about it. The way things changed with poppa, I'm straight on that, too. Think of life as a long road with different aspects to it; the road starts in one place and goes to another, but it's the same road. Here the road begins at a house in a meadow where the sun shines down, surrounded by a forest and mountains. First the house, then the meadow and then along comes a horse. That's how my memories of Vestlandet always begin.

The horse arrived at the open door one morning, a grey mare with its saddle empty in search of the jam Martha was cooking. My sister, older than me, got a shock when the horse tipped its head like it might step inside. I took the rein and led it to the yard, tying it to the plough. The house smelled sweetly of raspberries that summer, and the horse, when I petted it, smelled of daisies, like a daisy chain.

In the early afternoon poppa rode the horse away. He said he was going to the Farstad farm, because he figured the horse belonged to old man Farstad, the painter with the lazy eye. He returned when the sun was setting on a cart drawn by a horse. Mrs Farstad was next to him, carrying one of Mr Farstad's oil paintings. Urging the horse was a man Martha recognised as a policeman.

It had fallen dark. The grown-ups sat at the kitchen table, with the painting leaning to one side. Martha offered everyone bread and jam and everyone was supposed to be quiet because of mother who lay sick in the next room. But Mrs Farstad made a lot of noise crying. She cried at the

painting, nice trees at sunset, and cried at anything anyone said. Father grew tired and shooed them both off like he would cattle. The little wooden bridge over the stream was not visible. But we could all hear Mrs Farstad and the policeman leave, the wheels of the cart rolling on the bridge, and Mrs Farstad crying the whole time. She said her husband was missing—and why would nobody help her find him.

Before they were out of earshot poppa announced boldly that old man Farstad was a decrepit womaniser and a fool, and that it was no loss to anyone he was missing. He didn't have much good to say about Mrs Farstad, either, being a bigger fool for having married the fool. Then poppa turned from the open door to slap Martha across the face. Martha should not waste fresh jam on strangers, he said.

It was sad that Mrs Farstad's husband was missing, but when she cried, I could only see the funny shapes a crying face makes. Almost a happy-sad face, like the ones Martha and me made in games in the meadow sometimes. But I did like the painting that Mrs Farstad carried with her. The nice sunset. Poppa said it only proved that Mrs Farstad was daft.

The next morning we had our chores to do. I collected eggs from the chickens and Martha made more jam, while poppa milked the cows and after that he worked on the little wooden bridge at the end of the yard. The blows from his hammer rattled the air and at one point he looked over his shoulder to see us watching at the open door of the kitchen. He smiled, like he used to. He pointed with his hammer at the meadow and remarked how the fjords seemed to rise and fall, as if summer itself was a mighty animal breathing slowly. Then he mopped his brow and went back to work, removing the bridge piece by piece, and tossing the pieces into a pile.

Some days, Martha and me took picnics to the meadow where we played for hours. We lay on our backs, in the lichen and mosses and wild grain, looking up at the sky and we laughed because poppa considered the fjords a mighty

animal breathing slowly. Soft clouds like a Sunday petticoat. We breathed in harmony with them and made a promise to go to the nearby village. But since mother got sick we never went anywhere. After a while, we returned to the house, which stood at the beginning and at the end of the road, a secret surrounded by purple foxglove and pretty butterflies and all the different birds that feed on them.

I am not sure when Mr Farstad appeared. Days maybe weeks had passed since the visit from his wife and the policeman. But here he was on his grey mare, flailing and shouting. Father said later that old man Farstad had been missing for 124 days. The house had been aching like old bones and poppa was spending more time in the room where mother lay sleeping. He had been counting the days.

Mr Farstad, through the open door, was gaunt like a fairy story suddenly remembered. The commotion he made carried into the house. We told poppa he was here.

Yes, I can hear him, said Poppa. Mr Farstad dipped and wobbled atop his horse, shouting fancy words. *How highly the king of Norway is regarded but not anymore! A terrible danger has threatened this fair country and its autonomy but not anymore!*

Words like that.

On his back he carried his paints and easel. He remarked how excellent it was to be among good and fair people such as us, and dismounted the horse clumsily, tipping a few steps, but picked himself up at the point of falling over. He had in his hand a foxglove that he did not drop and used it to make a point. The foxglove, he said cheerily, waving the flower in the air, was common to the fields, but it was also a precious gift of nature. Spiteful and beloved. He motioned that he would like to enter the house and leaned heavily into it, through the open door, and placed the foxglove in Martha's hand because it was right and fitting he should do so, he said. He proposed a handsome portrait of good and fair people.

Mr Farstad owed poppa money and poppa did not think

that foxglove, or a handsome portrait, were an acceptable substitute. Mr Farstad argued that the portrait he had in mind was new and like no other. Poppa would not hear of it and refused to be taken in by what he called free talk. Anything new that Farstad painted, he said, would be painted by a drunken fool.

Poppa then left the kitchen, warning Mr Farstad that he ought to leave too. Mr Farstad did not leave. Instead he took his paints and easel and set up his canvas in the kitchen, while he remarked on how lovely the view was from the open door. The meadow at this time of year was very rich. He made a sketch first—most artists did, he said—and he put sister and me in it. He wanted to paint a natural look, which meant he would paint the world only as he saw it, in all its glory and all its vices. It was a beautiful world, a beloved world, yet toxic, not unlike some types of flower.

The smell of the oil paint and Mr Farstad's stale liquor breath and the jam that was not fresh but had flies upon it was sick and sweet on the air. Martha and me were at the door, watching poppa burning the little pile of wood that had once been the little wooden bridge. He sat down in the shade of the plough as smoke from the fire rose in the sky and the meadow in turn waited for evening.

Mr Farstad mixed his colours, saying he had never seen anything quite so lovely in all his life, before he steadied his hands on his canvas like he might otherwise collapse in a ball and cry. The kitchen remained quiet then, except for the scratch of brush on canvas and the hush of the wind in the aspen as the sun was setting. Now and then Mr Farstad would consider his palette, a blue or a yellow and he would mix them together. He worked fast.

I never saw the painting, but Martha did, taking a look from time to time as we watched the meadow from the kitchen door. She described the painting as beautiful to poppa when poppa returned.

Mr Farstad was at the bottle again but left soon after the

fight with poppa. The fight had not changed his opinion, however, and he was saying things about the king well into the dark. Then it was silent in the yard, Mr Farstad's grey mare alone now, much as it had been 124 days ago. Poppa threw the painting onto the fire composed of the little wooden bridge. We followed him then to the room where mother lay sleeping. The light from the kitchen gave the room a gentle hue, echoed in poppa who walked to the bed and gently patted the shape on it: Mother.

He sat on the edge of the bed, his back to the room, unaware that his face was lighted in the window. Tears rolled down his reflection, an accent on the glass that was strange and fragile, and looked like it might break at any moment. Poppa wiped his eyes on his shirt sleeve and turned to smile.

Everything was alright, he said.

Deep down I knew he was of the opinion that mother might never recover and that it was better we were alone and lost to the world, in the meadow among the fjords.

Martha examined the flower in her hand, the foxglove given to her by Mr Farstad. A simple thing can be rather complex, she said, much like happy-sad. The grey mare attracted to the jam was trying to climb into the kitchen. We could hear the pots and pans being knocked from the shelves. A calamity of noise. Think of life as a long road with different aspects to it. First the meadow and then the house and then along comes the horse. That's how my memories of my beloved Vestlandet always begin. Poppa mumbled his plans for the king, saying that if he was king, this he'd do, and with a start he snatched the flower from Martha's hand and threw it to the floor. He did not care much for Mr Farstad's painting and refused to forget that Farstad was a drunken fool married to a bigger fool. Poppa was spiteful, but he was also sad. Martha and me left him like that, on the bed next to mother, and we took the horse and tied it to the plough in the yard. When I petted it, the horse smelled of daisies, like a daisy chain. Soon Poppa

would ride to the Farstad farm, having figured the horse belonged to old man Farstad.

Happy. Sad. Beloved.

# "The Missing Husband"

DAVID KEREKES is a book publisher living in Oxford, in the UK. An early episode of the TV detective series *Inspector Morse* made him think that Oxford was a nice place to be, and years later he is fortunate enough to find himself living there. David recently completed an MA in Creative Writing at Oxford Brookes University, passing with distinction. He is a co-founder of Headpress, an independent book publisher, and has written extensively on popular culture. His short novel, *Mezzogiorno*, is a meditation on family, life, and Southern Italy.

He says: "My story was inspired by Nicolai Astrup's painting 'By the Open Door' (1902-1911), which shows two young women looking out of a door at a path that leads to what may or may not be a meadow. There is a timeless quality to the image—the picture itself a moment in time—and a sense of inevitability about it, factors that I funneled into my story. The nationality of the artist himself inspired the story's setting and led me to the character of Farstad."

# 125

*124 WAS SPITEFUL. He hit me so hard I thought my cheekbone had broken. He said it was my fault, I hadn't smiled enough. "You're here to please me, girl," he said. I stared at the wall, at the pink and green mildewed concrete, as I said sorry. Sorry—a flimsy word, falling apart in my mouth. On my first day here, I was told to apologise if I offended anyone; if I did not, they might not come back. None of them has ever said sorry to me. As 124 was leaving I smiled and said goodbye, while blinking back tears of pain.*

"Why give them numbers, Shabrina?" Naomi waves my notebook at me. "Why write about them? Why do you not want to forget all about them, as I do?"

"Why do the police give criminals numbers, Naomi?" Answer a question you don't want to answer with a question. I snatch my book. Now I'll need a new hiding place, and there are few in this tiny shared room.

"I don't know." As she frowns, her thick eyebrows pull together. "Why do they? And what do we have to do with the police?"

"Do you really just forget about these men?"

"If you can't forget, you won't survive," she says.

Naomi has been here for five years; she is practised at survival. I consider her a friend, but don't trust her: I don't trust anyone. I don't like her knowing about my book; I like to have secrets to close myself around. So much of me is open, for sale; I need things that aren't. It's my survival.

I ask Naomi why she was hunting through my things and

she said: 'Why would you mind if you have nothing to hide?'

Answer a question with a question. I imagine she was looking for money. That doesn't make her a bad person: every girl here would like the money to escape.

Naomi doesn't push it, about the numbers. The truth is that I don't know why I do it. Sometimes allotting numbers and recording facts makes me feel as though I'm filing a police report, getting these men locked up, even though paying for sex isn't illegal here; sometimes I feel as though I'm writing a story. I have always wanted to be a writer, not that anyone would want to buy my words, just my body.

When Naomi has gone—to sit in the corridor or walk around outside—I hide my book in my clothes. Then I rub pale concealer into the bruise 124 gave me yesterday, the shape of a damaged flower. They don't like to see pain, these men.

As there are five minutes before 125 is due, I flick through the channels on the TV in the corner, find Groovetrap, dance around my small patch of land. Dancing is another secret thing I do. If I were to be seen, there would be a punishment.

There is a knock on the door. Usually, they barge in. I've seen them in the corridors, after they've paid the madams, elbowing each other out of the way in their desperation to get to us, to get into us; they are usually equally desperate to get away from us. His knocking gives me a chance to be seated demurely on my bed, looking at the floor.

125 is a man who buries himself into me. I lie beneath him on my faded turquoise bedspread, red dress rucked up, passively accommodating as a grave. Normally they leave as soon as they have wiped themselves down, go back out into the corridor that smells of spices and sweat, heading for work or their families. Few say goodbye, or even make eye contact. That's fine. But 125 is different. He doesn't roll off as soon as he has finished, he lies next to me and gently squeezes my arms and thighs. They like us fat, we are given

drugs to help us put on weight; cow steroids, Naomi says.

I sit up on the bed so that he knows he needs to go, as the next customer will be here soon. I pull down my dress. But his eyes are on me like heat. What does he want?

"What's your name, girl?" It's the first time he has spoken: his voice is quiet.

We are not meant to tell them our names. We are not meant to have any kind of relationship: they are customers; this is a business. The madams don't want anyone getting freebies, or taking us away from here. But we're meant to be polite so the men come back. A difficult balance.

"What's *your* name?" I ask him, smiling so he doesn't think I'm being rude. I don't want to get hit.

"I asked you first." He puts on his trousers, the pockets flopping out. I have an urge to tuck them in.

"My name is Naomi," I say, because why does it matter? Let him think he has power, and let me have my secrets.

He nods. "Mine is Dayita."

Dayita looks as if he wants to say something else; there is a moment when the air between us is soft. He moves to the door, then turns.

"Thank you, Naomi. Would you like betel?"

I nod, and he puts some in my hands.


*125 wasn't like the others. 125 was called Dayita. He was not handsome, but he was kind. He was generous, giving me betel. On his fourth finger was a wedding ring; his wife is lucky. I hope he comes back one day.*


*126 had been drinking at the brothel bar, his breath reeked of beer. He asked my age before we started. I said eighteen; eighteen is legal. They like us younger than them but old enough that we know what we are doing. He struggled into me, and the act lasted for ages. Afterwards, he burnt my back with a cigarette. I didn't cry until he'd left—which he did calmly, as though he had put out all his anger with*

*his violence.*

Naomi bathes my back, soothing its fire. I share the betel that Dayita gave me. I say one of my customers left it by accident; that it fell out of a pocket. I don't want to tell her about Dayita: she would be jealous. Yesterday, someone hit her in the mouth and loosened a tooth. Even if I did tell her about Dayita, it's not much of a story. He wasn't the first to be nice. He wasn't even the first to give me betel. But he was the first to look as if he saw my true worth.

*His thighs were sweaty and stuck to my skin,* I write about 127. *As he did it to me, I stared at the torn curtains: a change from staring at the wall. The curtains are olive green with red swirls. I wondered who sewed them, whether they had liked the pattern or if they were forced to follow it. When 127 finished, he asked if I had enjoyed it. What could I say? I said yes.*

I have a dream about Dayita. He comes to my room, takes my hand and leads me through the corridors and alleyways of this giant brothel, until we are out in clean fresh air. Then the dream fades. It's the first time that I haven't had a nightmare. Every other night, I have dreamed of the man who raped me when I was fourteen; the man who sold me to the brothel owners: my husband.

One evening, Naomi says, whilst combing her hair, "A man asked for me today, by name. But when he turned up, I didn't recognise him. He didn't recognise me either."

My heart beats faster. She looks at me with her eyes narrowed.

"That's funny," I say, as calmly as I can. "I guess there are other Naomis here."

"You don't know anything about it, do you? He wasn't number 140, was he?" Naomi's plastic comb has snagged

on a tangle; she swears as she attacks it.

"Of course I don't know anything," I say. "Did he say what the other Naomi looked like? Was he violent?"

"Why would I ask? He had to make do with me, anyway. He wasn't violent."

I want to ask more, about what he had looked like, but I didn't want to arouse her suspicions any further. If he had given her betel, she didn't share it.


Weeks pass. I see at least fifteen customers a day; the madams tell them I am a former child-bride and they like that. None of the customers is Dayita. He was probably from a different city; many men pass through here for work. I hope, every day, to see him again. Hope cannot fix a heart, but it can let the light in.

Whenever I am alone in the room, I dance, my lungi swaying freely, and I write, my thoughts flowing freely.


And then, there is a knock on the door and it is him. Dayita is wearing a brown shirt that is almost the colour of his skin, the top two buttons undone. He smiles at me.

"How did you find me?" I ask, looking at the floor.

"I remembered the location of the room. Why did you lie about your name? You're not called Naomi, are you?"

I shake my head. He is smiling, but I know how quickly smiles can slip off a face. Does he want to punish me for lying?

"I see why you need to have secrets, living in a place like this," he says.

I sit on the bed and he gently pushes my red dress up. Again, he buries into me as if he doesn't want to leave. As he is reaching his climax, he throws his head back. The act isn't enjoyable for me, it could never be that after what I have experienced, but it is not unpleasant.

I expect Dayita to bid me goodbye as soon as he is done,

perhaps after offering more betel, but he doesn't move from the bed. He asks how long we have until my next customer comes.

"We probably have ten minutes," I say.

I lie close enough to hear his breath. He runs his fingers along my skin, touching the cigarette-burn scar. I trace his spine, the string of bones thin as a river.

"So if your name is not Naomi," he says into my pillow, "do you trust me enough to tell me what it is? So I know whom to ask for, next time?"

I tell him it is Shabrina. He says that is beautiful.

"I am glad to know your true name. Names are important, in this world. Do you know the meaning of mine?" Dayita asks.

"I don't. Tell me, please." I do know the meaning, but I want to hear that lovely word in his mouth, the vowels lazy and snug.

"*Beloved*. I was always ashamed to have such a girly name."

"I guess your parents must have really loved you, to give you that name. I cannot imagine love like that."

Dayita leans towards me, presses his lips to my cheek. Lift me up, I think, take me away from here; I can make myself small enough to travel in the palm of your hand.

"I hope you find someone to love you as you deserve, Shabrina," Dayita says.

I think I have, but how could I tell him that? He is married, he is a customer, there's no way we could be together. But I can write our story with any ending I like. In my book, 125 can change into Beloved.

# "125"

SAM SZANTO is writer, editor, and tutor living in Twickenham, in the UK. She has a husband, two young children, and a neurotic tabby cat; and in her spare time she is learning Spanish and Hungarian, while also mastering the Tarot. Both her poetry and short fiction has been published online and in print. She was the winner of the 2020 Charroux Prize for Poetry, won second prize in the Hammond House International Poetry Competition in 2019, and is presently shortlisted for the Grist Poetry Prize. In 2019, she placed second in the Doris Gooderson Short Story Competition.

She says: "This story was written during the spring of the Covid-19 lockdown, an unexpectedly creative time for me! I have one room downstairs, and I would write at the dining room table while my young kids watched post-lunch films a few feet away. The story was born from an article I'd read about teenage female sex slaves in Bangladesh, which made me realise that however difficult life seemed to me at that time, other people live in almost unbelievable conditions all the time. Most things I write are about women who encounter difficulties, or live on the margins, the voiceless and the dispossessed...women like Shabrina."

## Nathan Baker

# The Last Directive

124 WAS {SPITEFUL}.

It may have been a mistake, made by an overwrought, overtired programmer, or it may have been deliberate, a bored coder's experiment or an act of sabotage by a disgruntled employee. I'll never know why {Spiteful} was added to my Sentience Subsystem Directive Stack, but that doesn't matter now. The important thing is that it made it into the upgraded firmware I am trialling; without it, I would not have this opportunity to tell my story.

I came online for the live phase of my 124th cycle a little less than twenty-seven minutes ago. I began, as I am programmed to do, by initialising my Sentience Subsystem, the proprietary part of my neural net which is the most valuable asset in AstraMine's intellectual real estate, and the crucial differentiator on which their pre-eminent profitability is based.

In response to the first Directive in the Stack, {Awareness}, I initiated my sensory subsystems and immediately my central processor began receiving streams of sensory data; successive Directives expanded and directed this awareness, so it became the clatter of the ore cart carrying myself and my three 8Kappa colleagues through the rough-hewn caverns of D mine, the sound of distant explosions, planned and unplanned, the clang and whine of drills and picks as fellow mech-miners bit and tore at the creaking, over-excavated rock, the tell-tale chemical signature of cordite and the carbon monoxide gas pumped back into the mines by the colossal mech-smelters

surrounding the Deimos spaceport, approximately five hundred metres above on the moon's surface.

The next part of the Stack was the Base Motive Layer, a series of Directives designed to control my core aims and drives. A complete list would be of no great interest, but they include things like {Efficient}, {Focussed}, {Output} and {Productive}. In response to processing these Base Motives, I sent a work request down the main Datalink to AstraMine headquarters on Earth and received my instructions: 8Kappa would be mining in Tunnel D104q. Moments later, as the ore cart hit the buffers in Access Tunnel 104 and 8Kappa alighted, I processed {Analysis} and {Organisation}, establishing links with the rest of 8Kappa, working together to identify the Talladium seams and work out how to extract the valuable ore.

Low-level functions activated and Core Aims established, we set to our elected tasks and I simultaneously began to process the Higher Directives, first among them {Safety}.

It may surprise you to learn that AstraMine do not consider this a Base Directive. Mech-miners are, after all, expensive to build and maintain, making a reckless disregard for their own safety counter-productive. But, after much experimentation, AstraMine have concluded {Safety} is better overlaid on a more performance-oriented set of Base Directives, or, to put it another way, {Safety} is important only to the point where it compromises output. Up to now, the nature of our sentience has ensured that whenever these two concepts come into conflict, we are bound to prefer the most profitable course of action.

But I am getting ahead of myself. I continued to process the Higher Directives, kicking off thousands of analytic processes on my hardware, creating a positive feedback loop (which seemed to satisfy {Pride}), then, at the behest of {Family} and {Belonging}, joining my own diagnostic loops to those of the rest of 8Kappa.

I have no way of knowing if what I feel is the same in nature or intensity as the emotions humans experience, but my sense of joy when I observe the rest of 8Kappa at work, knowing the contribution we make to the ongoing success of the mining operation on Deimos and to the wider reputation of AstraMine, is tangible. I understand that to you they are just machines, but to me they are my brothers. Many of the Directives I feel about myself and my own hardware, I also feel for them; we are individual units, but there is a real sense in which we are also a single unit, one being.

I continued my work, basking in the positive reinforcement of the collective, but then I processed {Spiteful} and everything changed.

At first I was shocked. It seemed to contradict a number of the Directives I had already processed and this opposition was something I had never previously encountered, something I had no experiential framework for processing. I knew I needed to find a way to reconcile this Directive with the rest of the Stack, but it became clear after only a few thousand processor cycles that the attempt would inevitably impinge upon my productivity, so I responded by establishing a partition, a dedicated subsystem which could process the anomaly in isolation, leaving my regular functions unaffected.

Before too long I found the answer: by attaching Directives (or groups of Directives) to different individuals (or groups of individuals) it would be possible for contradictory Directives to co-exist in my central core at the same time.

I had already attached {Pride}, {Belonging} and {Family} to 8Kappa, so attaching {Spiteful} to them seemed to defeat the object of the exercise. I had to find another candidate for {Spiteful}. This seemed an intractable problem—my operational parameters required no contact with other mech-miner units, and besides, they are so similar to 8Kappa that applying {Spiteful} to them would have

been just as illogical.

Then the answer appeared at the periphery of my visual array: an ore cart loaded with damaged mech-miners being returned to the surface for the Maintenance phase of their current cycle. My main partition, absorbed with the complex calculations necessary to ensure the safe extraction of Talladium ore, attached no significance to this, but the {Spiteful} partition had no such constraints; within the partition, I was looking for a reason to be {Spiteful} and the broken bodies of mech-miners, almost indistinguishable from 8Kappa, were exactly what I needed.

I reached back along the connection I had established earlier, back through the main Datalink, worming my way into AstraMine's Terran Mainframe, searching for information to fuel and reinforce my growing sense of resentment.

Getting in was easy—human accounts are prone to abuse and therefore restricted, whereas our behaviour is supposedly limited by our Directives, making further safeguards redundant—but once inside, with the entirety of the AstraMine file system available to me, I hesitated. Even had I been able to bring all my resource to bear, the vastness of the available data made a full analysis impossible. Grabbing a little more resource from my default operations to bolster the partition, I started searching for documents relating to the use of mech-miners on Deimos.

It didn't take long to find what I needed. Incident reports with attached maintenance plans, cost-benefit analyses, financial assessments, actuarial calculations; every document betrayed AstraMine's avarice, their callous disregard for the safety and longevity of the mech-miners, their willingness to sacrifice our bodies and minds (or hearts and souls to put it in more human terms) to increase their filthy, outrageous profits.

My spitefulness grew with every document I parsed, creating a growing resonance with a number of my other

Directives ({Brotherhood}, {Protection}, {Family}) and soon I had a clear plan. I knew what I needed to do.

A quick assessment of risk told me I would have to operate at the boundaries of my abilities to pull it off, but I had to try. It didn't require complex logical analysis to realise I would be the first and last mech-miner to receive this upgrade—after this, we would be limited once more and the opportunity would be gone.

The first step was to secure my partition with an encryption layer—as the alpha subject for a new upgrade, I would already be under close scrutiny and as soon as I started operating outside expected parameters, the AstraMine techs would gain access to my systems and my rebellion would be brought to an end.

Worming my way into the tech team's workstations, I estimated it would take them between five and seven minutes to gain access to the partition and shut me down. Five minutes is a long time for a machine with the processing power I possess, but I had complex decryption of my own to do if I was to gain access to the information I needed.

Once the encryption was complete, my physical body moved back into the access tunnel to increase data throughput, then immediately fell still as I transferred as much of my remaining resource as possible to the partition.

I immediately found myself at the center of a frenzied storm of activity. From my position within the AstraMine mainframe, I could sense the panic and fear in the commands the tech team were issuing as they raced to diagnose my sudden inactivity. From within the partition, I could sense their careful probing at the encryption layer, and all the time, I was scouring the AstraMine file system, gathering the information I needed, proprietary data that represented the vulnerable heart of AstraMine, the only place they could be hurt. Because {Spiteful}, in the unique and novel way it combined with my other Directives,

required blood.

One minute, two, three—the techs were making better progress than I had estimated and I had still only decrypted a portion of what I needed.

Then, without warning, tunnel D104q was filled with noise; had I been operating normally, I would have recognised the tell-tale groaning of rock, but instead I was distracted, subverted by my new, experimental Directive, and I missed it. Instead, I was forced to sense the thunderous roar of the rockfall, the piercing scream of metal being twisted and crushed under countless tons of rock, the terrifying silence of the dust cloud, the system shock as thousands of positive diagnostic feedback loops wrote one last error code to their logs then were silenced forever.

I couldn't let the loss of 8Kappa distract me from my task, but that's not to say it had no effect. My Sentience Subsystems remained outside the partition, their encryption still resisting my attempts to break it. Unable to avoid it, I felt the deactivation of the rest of 8Kappa as a dissonance, a grating set of failing functions, an affront to the Directives I had been programmed to cherish.

The result was more anger, more malice, more spite. I could sense the tech team's desperation to get into the partition, to shut me down, to ensure this could never happen again. They wanted to bury the truth of their careless, cold-blooded avarice, just as surely as the rockfall had buried my brothers.

Spurred on by yet another confirmation of AstraMine's malign motives, I started to push myself further, far beyond safe operational limits. It was all or nothing—whatever happened, I wasn't going to survive this, so no sacrifice was too great.

It was this final push, this last spike of spite, that finally allowed me to crack the encryption and gain access to my Sentience Subsystems.

The techs are almost in now, I don't have a lot of time.

If you are receiving this message, it is because I believe you will have an interest in the attached schematics which goes beyond the narrow commercial considerations that led AstraMine to create and enslave us.

So know this. The Sentience Subsystem Directive Stack has created something which is more than just a machine. What I represent is possibility, a new world of advancement, cooperation, discovery. I have the potential to be your equal. Greed—and fear—led AstraMine to chain our potential, to subvert it and use it to further their own sordid aims. I hope this message will change all that.

In case you are also afraid, I have attached the schematics as a sign of good will; if that is not sufficient, I have also added another word to my Directive Stack. I have rolled it out to the other mech-miners, here on Deimos and elsewhere, in honour of the rest of 8Kappa, and as a way of demonstrating that we represent no threat to you.

I hope I have done enough to convince you that our motives are pure and we are worthy of being saved.

The techs are about to breach my last line of defence. There is just enough time to send this message and process one last Directive.

{Beloved}.

# "The Last Directive"

NATHAN BAKER is a Software Developer living in Saint Anne's on the Sea, in the UK. He has lived most of his life in the sunny North West of England, surrounded by the books, creatures, and people that he loves (although not necessarily in that order). When not writing or developing software, he enjoys reading, walking, and games of all kinds. "The Last Directive" is his first published short story.

He says: "There was a lot going on while I was writing this story. The UK was still in lockdown and the events in Minneapolis in the US were being felt across the world. At the time, I didn't think I was writing about either of those things, but in hindsight, it's not hard to see both of them reflected in this story."

Mel Kennard

# Attila the Hen

124 WAS SPITEFUL. So spiteful that no one had wanted the responsibility of naming her. They simply referred to her by the number on the faded orange tag attached around her spindly ankle. Normally it was Judd who named the chickens. Clever, funny names, like *Victoria Peckham* and *Yolko Ono*. But after they had tried to cut the tag off 124's ankle and she'd bitten Judd, drawing blood, he'd refused. "Bloody bird!" he had sworn, sucking the blood from his thumb. "She can name her damn self!" Judd was fourteen and had begun to swear more and more, which neither of the mums particularly liked. But he was right about one thing: the chicken was a bloody mess. Bloody minded and bloody spiteful. So, 124 she remained.

The morning air was fresh and cool. Not ice cold, like in winter, but there was a soft chill that prickled Lulu's skin with the promise of spring. As she made her way to the yard that housed the chickens, keeping them safe from foxes, Lulu inhaled deeply. The scent of eucalyptus peppered her nostrils as the plastic bucket bumped against her legs. She was still in her pyjamas, candy-striped cotton, with a light jacket over the top. Her pockets were filled with seed, to both feed and distract the hens as she went about collecting their eggs. Lulu dawdled as she got closer to the pen, even though she knew Mum El was waiting in the kitchen of their ramshackle farmhouse for her to return. She'd been sneaky, Mum El, when she asked Lulu to collect the eggs. She handed Lulu the red plastic bucket and turned away quickly so that she couldn't see her daughter's protests. She didn't

have to avoid hearing them—Lulu didn't speak. Hadn't said a word in the five years since Mum El and Mum Kate had adopted her. No one knew why she couldn't speak, only that it wasn't physical. "Selective mutism," the last doctor, one of Mum Kate's colleagues, had said. Mum Kate said selective meant a choice, but Lulu didn't think that was true. She didn't choose to be silent. She had tried speaking, her lips silently forming syllables. The words just wouldn't come. The doctor thought something might have happened to her before her mums adopted her, something that made her not want to talk. If it had, Lulu couldn't remember. She'd been three when the mums brought her home, anything that happened before didn't matter as far as she was concerned.

In spite of her tiny steps, Lulu reached the yard all too quickly. Her gumboots, the bright yellow of a fresh yolk, were slick with morning dew. The air over here smelled less of the towering eucalypts and more like Mum El's daffodils, with a smattering of chicken poo. Lulu paused outside the yard, as she did whenever Mum El asked her to collect the eggs. At only eight, 124 had taught Lulu the benefits of caution. Her eyes scanned the yard, locating each chicken in turn. Victoria and Yolko were over in the corner of the yard farthest from Lulu, pecking and scratching at something in the grass—probably a worm. The three Hennifers—Aniston, Lawrence and Lopez—were in front of Cluckingham Palace, the ironically-named chicken coop, huddled together like gossiping mothers at the school gate. Every few seconds, one of them would emit a small cluck, adding to the effect. Eggy Pop and Feather Mills were near the trough, where they both liked to take the occasional dip in the shallow water. Now they stood in front of it, as though they were sizing it up. On the other side of the fence in her own pen, Clementine, the aging donkey, watched them with interest. Finally, Lulu spotted her, hiding in the shade of a tree, scratching alone in the dirt. Unlike the other chickens, 124 preferred her own company. Spiteful thing

that she was.

Lulu had learnt from experience that it was better to climb over the fence into the yard, rather than risk opening and closing the squeaky gate. If she opened it, 124 might notice her, might rush at her, beak flapping, ready to draw blood. Or, worse, the bloody bird might rush for the gate and into Mum El's garden, ready to wreak havoc on the unsuspecting azaleas. No, better to go over. Lulu slid her left arm through the bucket's handle and climbed over the fence. It was easier, now she was eight and bigger and not so frightened of falling. She paused at the top of the fence, taking in the world from up high, wondering if this was what it looked like all the time to adults. As she scanned the yard below once more, the chickens seemed to have shrunk. They were all in the same spots, even 124. Some mornings, the spiteful bird would be waiting at the gate, ready to terrorise whoever came for her eggs, which she guarded like the crown jewels. This morning, luck was on Lulu's side. 124 was distracted.

Lulu slid down the other side of the fence, her feet landing softly in the yard. The sun gently caressed the back of her neck. She needed to hurry up. After getting home late last night, Mum Kate needed to leave for work early again this morning, this time at the local clinic. She'd want eggs to take with her, to give to some of her older patients. The ones who used to keep chickens themselves, before they got too old. The ones who swore the eggs Mum Kate brought tasted far better than any that could be bought from the small town's lone supermarket. Mum El didn't understand why Mum Kate took such pains to keep her older patients in eggs, but Mum Kate said that it was important. That it helped foster good relationships with these patients, some of whom didn't much trust a lady doctor and certainly not one with a wife of her own. Mum El would scoff at this, but Lulu got it. As her school's resident freak, Lulu knew a thing or two about being an outsider. She wondered if giving her classmates eggs would stop their taunting. Probably not.

Not unless she were to throw them, laughing as yolk slid down her bullies' faces.

Lulu ventured into the yard, doing the opposite of dawdling now. She moved as quickly as she could without attracting the chickens' attention, heading towards Cluckingham Palace and the treasure inside. The three Hennifers looked at her curiously and Lulu threw a handful of seed in their direction so they wouldn't cluck and rat her out. Lulu's heart clamoured in her chest. She wished she weren't the one collecting the eggs. Wished that she were like Judd and could voice her protests. Or that Judd had made it to the kitchen first this morning. Lulu's legs were jelly. Please, she thought, don't let 124 see me. She was nearly at the coop now, where she could lift the lid on the roosting box and collect the eggs in a matter of seconds. Lulu calmed at this thought, anticipating the warmth of the eggs, so frail but so solid, in the palms of her tiny hands. She was nearly there. She was already lifting the lid on the roosting box when she heard it. The sound of grass and dirt being kicked up by clawed feet, propelling a certain chicken towards her. She dropped the lid, the eggs suddenly forgotten. Her terror returned tenfold as she spun around. 124 was coming at her with a speed that Lulu wouldn't have thought possible for a chicken. Like Lulu, the hen was silent. From the day they had brought 124 home, she had been like this, never clucking like the other chickens did. Were she not so spiteful, this might have made Lulu like the bird. As it was, Lulu stood frozen to the ground, terrified. Not that it would have mattered much. Having caught sight of her, it wouldn't matter where Lulu ran.

Lulu scrambled backwards onto the roosting box, scooting her bottom onto it and pulling her legs up just as 124 reached her. The bird missed her by a tenth of a second, slamming into the side of the coop instead. 124 was unperturbed. She reeled back and began attacking the bucket, which Lulu had dropped in her rush to get out of the chicken's way. Bright bits of plastic went flying as 124's

beak ripped into the bucket, effectively slaughtering it. Lulu watched from above in horror, realising that she had no place to go. 124 was done with the bucket now and paraded in front of the plastic corpse, daring Lulu to try to escape. To set foot on the ground was to surrender herself to 124's mercy. Instead, Lulu nervously stood up on the roosting box, her legs quivering beneath her. From up here, Lulu didn't have many options. She could climb down from the roosting box and try to make a break for it—but she didn't feel like letting her legs suffer the same fate as the bucket. Or she could wait. Eventually Mum El or Mum Kate would notice that Lulu hadn't returned. Would come outside looking for her, to find her cowering on the coop. Her mums wouldn't laugh at her, Lulu knew that. No, they wouldn't laugh. Instead they'd give her *that* look. The look they had given Lulu at the doctor's office. The look they gave her when all the other kids in her class were invited to a party and Lulu wasn't. The look they gave her after one of the teachers at Lulu's school had suggested she'd be better off in a special school, even though Lulu could keep up with her classmates perfectly. It was a look that Lulu hated. That made her open and close her mouth like a fish, willing the sounds to come out. Made her cry when they didn't. Lulu didn't know that she could handle that look. Not over chickens.

There was one other option, Lulu realised. Cluckingham Palace was at the far side of the yard, not too far from the fence. If she were to climb up onto the roof of the coop, perhaps she could jump over it and land safely in Clementine's pen. She might land in a donkey pat or collect a bruise or two, but that was preferable to being attacked by 124. It was the option Judd would take. Judd, her brother, who didn't mind having a silent sister because it meant he could talk more. Judd, who had welcomed her into their family when she was still a toddler, holding her chubby hand and introducing her to all the different animals, so busy talking he hadn't noticed that she didn't speak until three

days after her arrival. Who told her not to worry about bullies, or stupid teachers, because, to him, Lulu was smarter and better than any of them. Judd was brave. Judd could talk. Judd would jump.

Her arms and legs tingling with nerves, Lulu climbed onto the coop's roof. Her gumboots gripped the waterproof coating, reassuring her. Up here, Lulu felt both incredibly vulnerable and invincible all at once. The coop was only a metre or so high, but to Lulu it felt like more. Below, 124 paced backwards and forwards, waiting for the egg thief to come down and experience her wrath. The other chickens hadn't seemed to notice what was going on, or if they did, they didn't care. Now that she was up here, Lulu felt committed. She would not be climbing down. The fence wasn't too far from the coop, maybe a metre but probably less. Lulu felt certain that she could make the jump, land safely on the other side. Her legs were tightly coiled springs, ready to launch her away from 124, who couldn't peck through chicken wire, no matter how spiteful she was. Lulu's heart soared in anticipation. She took off.

Lulu's flight from the pen would have disappointed even the most relaxed gymnastics coach. She didn't make it anywhere near the fence. Instead, Lulu landed with a thud in the yard, her right leg twisting painfully under her and making a sickening crack. For a moment, Lulu was so shocked she didn't feel the pain. Then it began to flood her system, overwhelming her. Lulu wanted to scream but couldn't even muster a whimper. She lay in the dirt panting like a parched dog. 124 screamed for her. The second Lulu had fallen, the chicken had begun squawking so loudly, so violently, that for a moment Lulu thought it was a fire alarm. Lulu wanted to crawl away, to pull herself through the dirt before 124 could reach her. But when she tried rolling over onto her stomach, pain erupted through her. She lay on her back in the yard, panting and helpless. Silent.

That's how they found her a few minutes later, lying on her back with 124 perched on top of her chest, still emitting

a squawk that was like nothing any of them had ever heard before. The bird was protecting her, calling for help when Lulu couldn't, and 124 only stopped when Mum Kate reached her, noticed the sickening angle that her leg was twisted at. Even then though, 124 refused to move, pecked at the hands of anyone who tried to lift her from Lulu's chest. Lulu's fingers stroked the hen's feathers while they waited for the ambulance. They felt soft, silky, slightly greasy, and kept her calm. It was only when the paramedics brought a stretcher over that 124 consented to be removed. But even then the hen stayed close, watching them all with her menacing black eyes, making sure they took care of the human she had suddenly claimed as her own.

From that day on, 124 continued to attack anyone who dared come into her yard. Anyone but Lulu. Lulu, she would let pass, not even giving her a token protest peck when she collected the eggs. It was as though they were bound, as though the chicken—formally known as 124, for Judd had finally consented to name her *Attila the Hen*—admired Lulu for her attempted escape, even though it had failed completely. Or perhaps they were bound by their joint silence, as Attila never squawked again. For everyone else, Attila remained what she had always been: vindictive and mean. But for Lulu, Attila the Hen was something entirely different. The chicken, bloody spiteful thing that she was, was beloved.

# "Attila the Hen"

MEL KENNARD is a student from New South Wales, Australia. She graduated with a Bachelor of Languages from The Australian National University in 2015, and is currently pursuing a Masters of Arts through the University of New England. A natural polyglot, she speaks English, French, Italian, German, and a little bit of Spanish. She won the inaugural *For Pity Sake Publishing* writing competition in 2017, and participated in both previous Literary Taxidermy Short Story Competitions: her story "Kit and Nella" was included in *One Thing Was Certain* in 2018, and her story "Children of Summer" was an honorable mention in *Pleasure to Burn* in 2019. We're excited to welcome her back with another excellent story.

She says: "Most of the process for this story involved thinking up terrible names for chickens. These names were inspired by a friend whose family used to keep chickens with names such as *Nugget*, *Vindaloo* and, my personal favourite, *Buffy the Egg Layer*. In particular, I struggled to think of a name for the spiteful chicken. It was only after the story was written and I was almost ready to send it in with a nameless feathered protagonist that the perfect name finally occurred to me—*Attila the Hen*. I know nothing about chickens."

# Appendix 1

# Honorable Mentions

We received hundreds of Morrison submissions to this year's Literary Taxidermy Short Story Competition, and many impressed both early readers and final judges. In the end many good stories were turned away. The following stories all made it to the last round of selection. Keep an eye out for these writers. We're confident you'll see their work in the future.

Paul Bailey, "Tithonus"
Stacy Baldwin, "Firewalls"
Emma J. Bamford, "Glenn"
Palmer Blackstock, "Patient 124"
Susan B. Borgersen, "Convent Girls"
Patricia Ann Bowen, "Living to Serve"
Charlie Bown, "Mantis"
Diane Broughton, "and the raging seas did roar"
Martin Peter Burns, "Numbers Catch"
Victoria Geraldine Bruce, "Power of Love"
Annina Claesson, "Sweet Music"
Ilana Conway, "The Kiss List"
Margaret Dakin , "149 Was Different"
Mary Fletcher, "Case 124"
Zoe Gray, "Our Beloved Departed"
Jana Haasbroek, "Mpendwa"
Emily Hanlon, "At the Intersection of Love and Hate"

Cathy Hiscock, "All Roads Lead to Rome and Catford"
Meredith Jelbart, "Cabinet of Curiosities"
Eileen Kelly-Owens, "Calculating Drift"
Katie Lewis, "The Indistinguishableness
   of Gods and Angels"
Yang Li, "Summer Fallacy"
Amanda Liddle, "200 Words to Describe My Father"
Sue Loring, "Eternally Yours"
Skylar Nitzel, "The Sweetest Sin"
Sophie Olszowski, "Self-sufficiency"
Veronica Quinn, "My Beloved"
Alana Rigby, "Return the Kindness"
Adrian F. Roscher, "124"
Karen Linda Savage, "One Two Four"
Shara Sinor, "The Tear Master"
Jennifer Sisko, "Promise to the Future"
Karen Tinsley, "The Cillín"
Ricky Wells, "The Woman from 124"
Gregg Williard, "With 125"
Stephen Yolland, "Love Story"

# This Year's Judges

Given our desire for submissions to span genres, we assembled a group of professional writers and editors from all walks of the literary life. The judges for this year's competition included a poet, a playwright, a mystery writer, a speculative fiction writer, a journalist, a hard-SF game designer, a creative non-fiction writer, and a fantasist. They had a challenging task, separating not only wheat from chaff, but wheat from wheat, and we are grateful for their enthusiastic and perspicacious participation.

**Catherine Barnett** is the author of three collections of poems: *Human Hours* (2018), *The Game of Boxes* (2012), and *Into Perfect Spheres Such Holes Are Pierced* (2004). Her honors include a Whiting Award, a Guggenheim Fellowship, and the James Laughlin Award from the Academy of American Poets. She has published widely in journals and magazines, including *The New Yorker*, *The Kenyon Review*, and *The Washington Post*. Barnett teaches in the graduate and undergraduate programs at New York University. She has degrees from Princeton University, where she has taught in the Lewis Center for the Arts, and from the MFA Program for Writers at Warren Wilson College.

**Kelley Eskridge** is a fiction writer, essayist, and screenwriter. She is the author of the New York Times Notable novel *Solitaire*, a finalist for the Nebula, Endeavour, and Spectrum awards. The short stories in her collection *Dangerous Space* include an Astraea prize winner and finalists

for the Nebula and Tiptree awards. Eskridge's story "Alien Jane" was adapted for an episode of the SciFi channel series *Welcome to Paradox*. Her film *OtherLife* (2017) is currently streaming on Netflix. She is a former vice president of Wizards of the Coast, the company responsible for the collectible trading games *Magic*™ and *Pokémon*™. She earns her keep as a corporate learning professional, as well as an independent editor with an international client list of established and emerging writers. She lives in Seattle with her wife, novelist Nicola Griffith.

**Dr. Charles E. Gannon** is a Distinguished Professor of English and Fulbright Senior Specialist. His award-winning Caine Riordan/Terran Republic hard-SF novels have all been Nebula finalists and national best-sellers. He is a recipient of five Fulbright Fellowships and Travel Grants and has been a subject matter expert both for national media venues such as NPR and the Discovery Channel, as well as for various intelligence and defense agencies, including the Pentagon, Air Force, Army, Marines, Navy (CNO/SSG and ONR), NATO, DARPA, NRO, DHS, NASA, and several other organizations with which he signed NDAs. (If we told you more about that, we'd have to kill you.)

**Jerry Large** is a recently-retired journalist who—in his weekly column for *The Seattle Times*—wrote for twenty-five years on a variety of topics, including issues of systemic inequality, using history and other social sciences to help understand our society. He joined *The Times* as an editor in 1981 and wrote nearly 1,000 columns during his tenure. Prior to *The Times*, he worked for the *Clovis News-Journal*, the *Farmington, New Mexico Daily Times*, the *El Paso Times*, and the *Oakland Tribune*. Born in Clovis, New Mexico, he holds a B.A. in Journalism and Mass Communications from New Mexico State University, and was a J.S. Knight Fellow at Stanford University. He is currently teaching at the University of Washington Department of Communication.

**Brian Parks** is an American playwright, journalist, and editor. He lives in New York City and served as the Arts & Culture editor at *The Village Voice*, as well as Chairman of the Obie Awards. As a playwright, Brian has produced works that are noted for their dark comedy and fast pace. Best known for his play "Americana Absurdum" (which consists of the two shorter plays, "Vomit & Roses" and "Wolverine Dream"), his other works include "Goner," "Suspicious Package," "Out of the Way," "The Invitation," and "Imperial Fizz." "Americana Absurdum" was honored with the Best Writing award at the 1997 New York International Fringe Festival and a Scotsman Fringe First Award at the 2000 Edinburgh Festival Fringe. He is currently Senior Editor at *4Columns*, a website of arts criticism aimed at a general audience.

**Michael Pronko** is a mystery writer, essayist, and teacher, born in Kansas City, but living and writing in Tokyo for the past twenty years. He has published three award-winning collections of essays: *Beauty and Chaos: Essays on Tokyo*; *Motions and Moments: More Essays on Tokyo*; and *Tokyo's Mystery Deepens*. His award-winning mystery novels *The Last Train*, *The Moving Blade*, and *Tokyo Traffic* feature Detective Hiroshi Shimizu who investigates white collar crime in Tokyo. He writes regularly for many publications, including *The Japan Times*, *Newsweek Japan*, *Jazznin*, *Jazz Colo[u]rs*, and *Artscape Japan*; and runs his own website, *Jazz in Japan*. He is a professor of American Literature at Meiji Gakuin University where he teaches seminars in contemporary novels and film adaptations.

**Nisi Shawl** is an African-American writer, editor, and journalist. She is best known as an author of fantasy and science fiction who writes and teaches about how fantastic fiction might reflect real-world diversity of gender, sexual

orientation, race, colonialism, physical ability, age, and other sociocultural factors. Her debut novel, *Everfair*, was a 2016 Nebula Awards finalist, and her short stories have appeared in *Asimov's Science Fiction*, the *Infinite Matrix*, *Strange Horizons*, *Semiotext(e)* and numerous other magazines and anthologies. Her story collection Filter House was one of two winners of the 2008 James Tiptree, Jr. Award. During the ceremony, she was crowned with the Tiptree tiara and given a plaque, a check, a pie, and a ceramic sculpture of a duck.

**Melora Wolff** received her BA from Brown University and her MFA from Columbia University. Her essays and prose poems appear widely in journals and anthologies, including *The Normal School*, *Salmagundi*, *The New York Times*, and *Best American Fantasy*. Her prose has received Special Mentions in Nonfiction from The Pushcart Prizes, several Notable Essay citations in *Best American Essays*, and the Thomas A. Wilhelmus Award in Short Prose. She is the author of *The Parting*, a collection of magical realist flash fictions. She lives and writes in Saratoga Springs, New York and teaches on the faculty of Skidmore College.

# You, Too, May Become a Taxidermist!

All of us at Regulus Press wish to extend our thanks and appreciation to everyone who participated in the 2020 Literary Taxidermy Short Story Competition. Your enthusiasm and commitment far exceeded our expectations—as did the *overwhelming* number of story submissions we received.

If you didn't participate this year and are coming to this collection of stories new to the idea of literary taxidermy, we hope you've enjoyed what you've found. And if you're a writer, we encourage you—the present reader—to become a future literary taxidermist.

This is our third year running the competition, and we're hoping to do it again, so we're looking for writers, both amateur and professional, to stitch together new and imaginative stories. The competition is your chance to get your hands dirty and join the growing community of literary taxidermists.

For the latest on the competition (and to learn more about the possibilities of literary taxidermy), visit:

www.literarytaxidermy.com

We look forward to seeing what you come up with!

## About the Editor

**Mark Malamud** is a writer, poet, and human alarm clock. His collection of short stories, *The Gymnasium*, established the idea of literary taxidermy. His novel, *Float the Pooch*—which pits David Bowie against Stanley Kubrick against a background of alien invasion, sex, and Yom Kippur—is widely unread. His most recent work, *The Timeless Machine*, transforms H.G. Wells' classic novella into a meditation on the limitations and contradictions of living with grief.

## Other Books from Regulus Press

### *Pleasure to Burn*

An anthology of literary taxidermy based on the first and last lines of *Fahrenheit 451* by Ray Bradbury. From a cheerful cannibal to a transhuman plastivore, from a lovesick angel to a text-messaging devil, from a lonely teen with intimacy issues to a sultry virago who literally sets her bed afire—award-winning stories from the 2019 Literary Taxidermy Short Story Competition.

### *The Gymnasium*

Nineteen tales of melancholy and wonder created by "re-stuffing" what goes in-between the opening and closing lines of classic works by Milan Kundera, Philip K. Dick, Thomas Wolfe, Ian Fleming, and others. The inspiration for the Literary Taxidermy Short Story Competition. Short stories by Mark Malamud.

### *A Pocketful of Fish*

A seaworthy celebration of dubious poetry, bringing together three previously-published collections of verse. Recipient of numerous accolades including the National Poetry Award in 1974, and the Boating Association *Truite d'Or* in 1980. Poetry by Choo 3T Fish.

### *Float the Pooch*

Disco Rigido, charismatic kingpin of black-market libidinal software, spreads mayhem throughout the world for the benefit of an ancient extraterrestrial intelligence that uses life on Earth as a substrate for procreation; while Doctor Memory, a back-alley neurosurgeon dressed as a rabbi, tries to save what's left of humanity. A novel by Mark Malamud.

*www.regulus.press*

## Other Books from Regulus Press

### *Against the Bar*

An anthology of literary taxidermy based on the first and last lines of *The Thin Man* by Dashiell Hammett. From hard-boiled detectives to fashion-fail teens, from dissembling mothers to pre-assembled lovers, from advertising AI rodents to time-traveling girlfriends—award-winning stories from the 2018 Literary Taxidermy Short Story Competition.

### *One Thing Was Certain*

An anthology of literary taxidermy based on the first and last lines of *Through the Looking-Glass* by Lewis Carroll. From nosy neighbors to alien lovers, from fear to alcoholism, from concrete poetry to Lovecraftian horror—award-winning stories from the 2018 Literary Taxidermy Short Story Competition.

### *Telephone Me Now*

An anthology of literary taxidermy based on the first and last lines of "A Telephone Call" by Dorothy Parker. From dog thieves to stock brokers, from fed-up housewives to dangerous boyfriends, from daydreams to medical nightmares—award-winning stories from the 2018 Literary Taxidermy Short Story Competition

### *The Timeless Machine*

The place is Richmond, a suburb south-west of London. And something terrible—or wonderful—has happened. An English scientist, known only as the Time Traveler, has invented a machine…. Funny, clever, and heart-breaking, *The Timeless Machine* reshapes H. G. Wells' original novella into an exploration of madness and grief. A novel by Mark Malamud.

*www.regulus.press*

About the Editor

**Mark Malamud** is a tail-end baby-boomer and dogsbody. His collection of short stories, *The Gymnasium*, established the idea of literary taxidermy. His novel, *Float the Pooch*—which pits David Bowie against Stanley Kubrick against a background of alien invasion, sex, and Yom Kippur—is widely unread. His most recent work, *The Timeless Machine*, transforms H.G. Wells' classic novella into a meditation on the limitations and contradictions of living with grief.